Journey Through

DREAMS

S. AMOS

authorHOUSE®

AuthorHouse™ UK
1663 Liberty Drive
Bloomington, IN 47403 USA
www.authorhouse.co.uk
Phone: 0800.197.4150

Published by AuthorHouse   11/26/2018

ISBN: 978-1-7283-8143-5 (sc)
ISBN: 978-1-7283-8144-2 (hc)
ISBN: 978-1-7283-8142-8 (e)

Library of Congress Control Number: 2018913933

Print information available on the last page.

It was an August Saturday. She didn't have to go to the office today, but these days it was unimportant whether it was Saturday or not because since her illness she could only work when she felt able.

Amelia sat at her kitchen table gazing at the rambling countryside before her. Trees whose leaves were just on the turn bordered her landscape. Soon they would be golden yellow and it would be a whole year since she had moved into the country.

The orchards were heavily laden with apples. She wondered how they would be harvested. Would the farmer employ asylum seekers to pick the orchards and would they inflict noise on this quiet piece of heaven?

She daydreamed over her coffee. Amelia Stanton was in her mid-fifties, somewhat overweight but retained her soft, pale skin which she considered her only asset. She was, indeed, attractive but never thought so. A wicked Irish humour which had been suppressed over these last long three years, still was evident. More often than not, she was unable to concentrate, didn't like noise, wanted more than anything to escape from all her responsibilities. Her doctor called it depression.

One could argue that she had fewer responsibilities nowadays. She made another coffee. Amelia drank decaffeinated coffee because Dr Atkins had recommended so, as she was trying to lose weight.

The sound of a plane flying overhead startled her. She placed her cup on the top of a pile of books and moved to the kitchen window. The plane disappeared over the hill as she wondered where it might be travelling and imagined herself far away in Kyrenia thirty years ago. It was March in the early seventies and at the age of twenty-one she ran away with a married man. He was twenty years older than she and it all happened so quickly; the decision for him to leave his wife for Amelia and for them to elope. In a way it sounded rather romantic but there was no romance in their relationship.

Amelia was then young and attractive and wanted adventure. Having an affair was fun. It was fun meeting in carparks and switching cars to drive away to the coast for the weekend to sail, fish and have nights in the pub with the locals, then go to the cottage and make love for most of the night.

She had been on the employment books of the staff agency for a long time and still hadn't met the glamorous model, Mrs Black, who ran it. Her 'interview' had taken place over the telephone and she was engaged purely on the sound of her voice!

She was given an assignment, taking Amelia to a large factory on the industrial estate at Sturtonport. Having been able to secure a loan, Amelia had purchased a turquoise Mini car with white roof. This enabled her to travel to assignments all over the county. It was easily recognisable by the plastic stick-on flowers which she had arranged all over the bonnet, sides and roof of the little car. It was fun and that was what she was after. However, her pursuit of fun may well have been mistaken by other, perhaps not so outrageously outgoing people she would meet during the course of her work.

She parked the Mini in the staff car park at the large engineering factory and walked towards the reception area where two receptionists (acting telephonists) were sitting behind a glass screen wearing headphones.

Introducing herself as a 'temp' Amelia was quickly shown to the place where she would be working for the next month as a secretary to the New Products Manager.

The office was situated to the side of a long open-plan office, the walls of which were screened by obscure glass. One small desk was placed at an angle in the corner with chairs in front and behind. A number of filing cabinets were placed against the glass wall and a Pirelli calendar was pinned crookedly behind the desk revealing a pinup wearing only a scarf.

A tall, middle-aged, tousle-haired fellow with a broad grin ran up the corridor to meet Amelia, taking her hand, shook it with fervour. He bounded around like a baby on Lucozade taking her into his tiny office to outline her job description as accurately as possible. It was a position demanding a lot of technical explanations which Amelia would have to decipher. She took it in her stride knowing that she was good at what she did know and eager to learn more.

Amelia found Michael Hemmings very childish. He was a hungry leech who had already set his sights on her. He was hoping to devour her.

He removed the courtesy board on the desk to enable him to stretch his legs out fully underneath when Amelia was called to take dictation. He would 'accidentally' knock her foot. This move then accelerated to the removal of his shoe whereupon he brushed his socked foot between her legs. She was confused. She didn't know whether she was flattered at these advances. After all, she had just been rejected by the most wonderful man she had ever met. Now, someone appeared to find her attractive. She didn't know whether to respond, or to reject these advances so made no reaction initially.

Dissatisfied with her lack of recognition to his advances, Michael proceeded to dictate outrageous letters containing innuendoes typically disparaging. On one occasion when sending a sample of reinforced fibre-glass to a potential customer, he marked the sample as *"Best Shag."*

His demeanour was tall and slightly bent because of his height. Amelia's job was to help him with the backlog of work; instead, they discovered a magnetism coupled with a penchant for fun. Her abilities as a shorthand writer had taken her into courts as a verbatim reporter but speed wasn't required whilst working for Michael. In fact, he could take all morning to dictate a thank you letter!

Very quickly she had accepted his invitation for a weekend away at his cottage in North Wales. After finishing duties at the office early on Friday evening, he would meet her and they then travelled together in his car for a few days of fun. Michael was regarded as an eccentric millionaire by the local Welsh fishermen with whom they drank at the local pub. They all knew his wife yet kept tight lipped about Michael's frolics.

Midnight salmon fishing with the local fishermen turned out to be a skinny-dipping exercise, skipping over the nets and trying not to get tangled up whilst drawing in the catch. Downing pints at the pub till closing time and singing Land of My Fathers until they couldn't stand, was all part of being mistress for the weekend.

After a particularly raucous few days away, Amelia arrived at the office just a little worse for wear. When Michael told her that he had left his wife and booked two tickets to Nicosia, she froze. This was not what she had wanted. She didn't love him. She didn't want to live with him. She found herself finding faults with him. He was arrogant at times and loud. He was wealthy but mean. The age gap was vast and the generation differences would be difficult for her to undertake on a full-time basis. She did not want this to happen.

Not only was he walking out on his wife and four children, but also walking out on his job. His career would be in shreds.

Amelia tried to reason with him. She told him how it was better to continue as they did having the discreet weekends together. Where would they stay in Nicosia? Would it be permanent and if so, what would be the repercussions? There were too many questions and not enough answers.

This was all too much for Amelia to digest and without the answers, stepped into oblivion, packed up her belongings, gave notice on her apartment and prepared for an adventure that she had not expected. The only difference between the fun adventures they had shared together in the past, was that this was serious business and Amelia was just not a serious person.

Michael left his car in a long stay car park and headed towards East Midlands Airport where they caught their flight to Nicosia.

Amelia was just going through the motions of a dream. This was unreal. It was to be so consequential. They were taking it too far and she was afraid.

She slept on the plane whilst Michael shuffled papers from his briefcase. He appeared to have given this whole situation more thought than Amelia had had time to do.

Nicosia was pleasantly warm in March. Once through the customs, not knowing which direction to take they decided to head north and hopped on to an old bus which had "Κερύνεια" written on a piece of card hanging from the driver's windscreen next to a dangling rosary and a statue of Mary.

There were only four others on the bus. The driver started it up, tickled the accelerator causing the engine to roar and black smoke to belch out of the exhaust at the side, blackening the view for several seconds. After blessing himself with the rosary and kissing a palm cross, they began their mystery tour.

Amelia was afraid when, at the borders, they were confronted by UN soldiers in their familiar blue berets, yielding guns. Two soldiers mounted the steps of the bus, guns in the air demanding to see passports but once they had been vetted as tourists, they were able to continue their journey through beautiful countryside to the coastal harbour town of Kyrenia.

Fruit trees laden with grapefruit, lemons and oranges coloured the roadside. Every now and then they passed a child sitting on a chair under an umbrella, waiting to sell the fruit from the dusty verge. And, more than once, they saw a hideous blown-up dog left at the side of the road. Having died, the heat had caused them to inflate like balloons.

Once Michael and Amelia arrived at the coast and entered the town of Kyrenia, they disembarked the old bus, thanked the driver for a safe journey and walked up and down the narrow streets carrying their heavy luggage until they found a small hotel in a side street checking in as Mr and Mrs Michael Hemmings. Amelia felt slightly uncomfortable about pretending to be married as she wasn't wearing a ring and thought that might be noticed by the hotel owner. She remembered to keep her left hand out of sight whilst at the reception and left the signing of the register to Michael.

The hotel owner/porter/waiter/receptionist (and probably chef) was a large Greek man, presumably in his fifties, with olive skin and deep folds in his face where the exposure to sunshine had hardened his skin. He smiled and showed the gold caps on his teeth. Neither Michael nor Amelia could speak Greek nor Turkish, so their communication was limited to Theo's broken English. His large grubby hands turned the blank pages of a book then, with a sharp pencil, he scribbled their names across a new page. He didn't ask for passport details which was a relief for Amelia, although Michael didn't seem to be particularly interested.

"I show you where you are!" smiled Theo.

Being such a stickler for correcting Amelia for the least thing, she was surprised that Michael hadn't corrected Theo on his grammar.

The hotel was dark and cool as he showed them up the large marble staircase to a small room at the rear of the hotel. The room was warm despite a ceiling fan struggling to keep the air cool. Building works were taking place outside so the noise of machinery was way above the decibels limit which hadn't come into the law books at that time. Drilling work shook the walls of the room. Strangely the noises made the temperature of the room appear to be hotter than perhaps it was.

They were exhausted and wanted to take a bath as there was no shower, but to their great disappointment they found that there was no water either! The bathroom was outdated and quite some distance from the room. Later Mr Theo explained that to have the warm water you must use it at 6am. After that there was none! He failed to say how many other guests would be using the bathroom before them!

Taking that on board, they went for a stroll to escape the heat and noise, stopping at one of the street bars for some refreshment. Old men, sitting under the shade of the huge cypress tree in the square, were concentrating at playing cards whilst others fingered their worry-beads, supping brandy sours all day and into the early hours.

Michael and Amelia were given a demonstration on how to make the best brandy sour in Cyprus. Another Theo (whom they named Young Theo) took great pride in showing them how to sugar the top of the glasses by moistening them first with lemon juice, then placing the glasses upside down into a dish of sugar. Once the glasses were prepared they were filled with ice, then a very large shot of local brandy was poured over it, followed by a small amount of lemon juice topped with soda, cucumber slices and half a lemon. Lemons were large and plentiful, being sold at the side of the road having been freshly picked from the trees that morning.

Not knowing how long they were to stay, Michael and Amelia agreed that they couldn't remain in that awful room for any period of time and looked for a cheap villa where they could continue their "hiding". Eventually a female property agent called Melaina found them just what they wanted on the edge of the town. They had stumbled across her tiny office at the end of a narrow, cobbled street and were given a welcome to match no other when they popped their heads into the dark room.

Melaina was a tiny woman, smartly dressed with beautiful soft olive skin. Her shiny black hair fell down her back and across her forehead. Fond of gold, she wore it around her neck, on all fingers, in her ears and even sported rings on her bare toes. She listed their requirements on a scrap of paper torn from the corner of a book. Although she might have appeared a bit chaotic, she was very quick to find them the accommodation for which they had asked. Perhaps she owned it, they would never know.

Although basic, the villa was spacious and cool with marble floors and a delightful garden. They took it for three months during which time they would really get to know each other well.

Michael signed a piece of faded paper and handed over the cash deposit which Melaina counted twice to be sure that it was the correct amount. She reached over her cluttered desk and stamped another sheet of paper then signed it. The deal was apparently done so she put the cash in her handbag, slung it over her shoulder showing them the door as she gave Michael the keys.

When they left the hotel, Theo wanted to know where they were going to stay. Michael didn't hesitate in providing Theo with a forwarding address. They said their goodbyes thanking Theo as they carried their bags to the next street where they would be living in their first "home."

The villa was a single storey white painted concrete building, the only door being located at the back of the property with no access to the road other than by the path alongside the east wall. A somewhat dilapidated picket fence marked the boundary with the villa next door. The large overgrown, south-facing garden extended about 50 metres. A small patio area with old wooden table and bench were positioned directly in front of the only door.

The kitchen was large and basic. There was only a small fridge and single hot plate which had to be plugged into a broken socket near the door. A screwdriver had been pushed in the socket to act as a make-shift conductor for the earth.

There was a choice of two bedrooms. One with a double bed and the other with two singles. Only the one bedroom had a wardrobe. The other had a ceiling fan and window blind so they opted to sleep in that room shoving the two single beds together.

Amelia unpacked a few necessities and made herself familiar with the kitchen as she imagined that was the room in which most of her time would be spent!

The table was placed in the centre of the kitchen with only two chairs. They weren't expecting visitors so that was acceptable. The place really needed a good clean. Dust was thick on the kettle which she assumed was boiled on the top of the single ring hob. No cleaning equipment could be found in the cupboards so she began making a list of things she needed to get from the shops.

It wasn't long before a routine was established. In the mornings, before the days became too hot, they walked into the town to purchase fresh fish, vegetables and fruit according to their needs for the day unless they were travelling out of town.

The shops were hardly distinguishable from the street. Some might have a chair outside but the goods were always hidden away in long, dark rooms badly lit usually with a single fluorescent light often hanging from the cables attached to a beam. No prices were displayed on anything as the Greeks' method of buying was to banter or barter. Amelia had no doubt that they were overcharged, but accepted that that was the way it was.

It was when Amelia prepared the food that Michael became dissatisfied. He enjoyed eating and drinking the local wines which were frightfully cheap, but attempted to show Amelia how she should cook, how she should wash the dishes and place them strategically on the draining board. Because she just plonked them in a bunch to dry, it annoyed him intensely and led to them having their first disagreements.

She cooked the fish for too long – it was dry despite Amelia throwing lashings of packet sauce over the top. It was difficult enough cooking on only one hotplate but Michael didn't consider that.

Amelia noticed that Michael was very easily annoyed by very insignificant occurrences. He would leave her in the villa for hours whilst he went on long walks. He would drink in the bars and arrive home expecting her to want to bed him.

She became more and more unhappy. It was not acceptable in those days for a woman to drink in a bar alone. She felt trapped and wanted to return home but she had given notice so her apartment would not be available to return to. Michael had paid the full rental on the villa and was determined to stay it out and get his money's worth. He would not leave the island. Besides, he had burned his boats at home. He had nowhere else to stay. His wife didn't know his whereabouts and his pride would not allow him to return to her. He didn't want to admit that he had made a mistake. What could he do? If he pocketed his pride and went back to his wife, his life would be hell for ever more. She would never sleep with him again. He would have a sexless marriage and therefore would need to seek it elsewhere. It would be risky because she wouldn't trust him again. She was wealthy in her own right so didn't actually need him. He was in a dilemma. He had walked out of his job without saying a word so his career had abruptly ended.

Michael and Amelia decided to make the best of it. They hired a car and travelled the width and breadth of the small island.

They found miles of white sand beaches and golden rocks, totally uninhabited. They swam naked in the clear blue warm waters of the coast and played hide and seek amongst the rocks. They made love in the sand and washed again in the sea. They spent hours frolicking and cavorting, laughing and singing in oblivion. No-one could see nor hear them. This was heaven on earth – solitude at its best.

This was the cement in the relationship. They were otherwise incompatible. Whilst the domestic side of living together wasn't working, the sexual side certainly was fun!

Another time they visited Paphos and fed the pelican which roamed freely through the only street. Having a typical Greek lunch with lots of small dishes of mezze and drinking beer looking across the expanse of clear blue water, one could mistake the couple for a father and his daughter spending quality time together.

One morning, Amelia was clearing away the breakfast things when Theo arrived at the door.

"Kalimera, Theo. Póso oraío na se do. éla mésa." Amelia proudly showed off the little Greek she had learned. She was pleased to leave the washing up until later and invited Theo to sit at the kitchen table.

"Oh, Mrs Hemmings I bring you letter from England," Theo thrust the small blue envelope on to the table.

Amelia's stomach turned over. Who knew they were here, in Cyprus? Michael had gone for one of his walks, so she made tea for Theo and he stayed for a while, chatting in his broken English. Amelia didn't hear a word. She was in England, trying to imagine who would write to her. She looked at the airmail envelope and noticed that it was actually addressed to Michael. Would he reveal the contents, or should she try to open it carefully so that he wouldn't know she had read it?

She didn't have time to decide because Michael walked in and Mr Theo immediately reached over and took the envelope, handing it to Michael with a big gold grin saying,

"Mr Hemmings, I bring to you this from England. I give it to Mrs Hemmings cos I think you are not here."

Michael took the envelope without thanks and saw Theo to the door. Amelia collected the cups and returned to finish the washing up.

Michael was quiet and opened the envelope in the garden, away from Amelia. She could see him from the window as she drew the water in the kitchen sink. He paced up and down with his head down, pulling his fingers through his long hair.

Amelia tapped on the window. "Is everything ok?" she enquired.

Michael didn't look up and continued to pace up and down the garden path.

"Coffee?" called Amelia, "Turkish or instant?"

Michael kicked open the door with his foot and came indoors mumbling, "Oh, anything! Whichever you are making!"

"Who sent us a letter?" she asked.

"Who has sent ME a letter?" corrected Michael.

"Sorry!" replied Amelia as she picked up the coffee pot.

Michael made no attempt to discuss the letter with Amelia. She poured the coffee and they remained silent. She would have to observe his every move and see where he put it so that she could read it secretly when he wasn't around.

Michael was quiet for the rest of the day. Later, in the early evening they took a stroll around Kyrenia harbour and went to The Dome for a brandy sour. It was cool inside The Dome and they were able to talk politely with another English couple for half an hour or so. Meanwhile, Michael remained tight-lipped about the letter.

Amelia was almost bursting with anxiety. She really needed to know the contents of that airmail letter even moreso now than before, if only for the fact that Michael would not share the news.

At breakfast Michael didn't speak. Amelia presented him with half a melon fresh from the market that morning. She had been out early to get fresh fruit and vegetables. Michael didn't go with her. He chose to stay in bed which was unusual.

He began to cut the fruit and then laid down his spoon. He finished his coffee in one gulp and left the table.

"What is it?" asked Amelia as she ran after him. He shook her arm off his and walked to the end of the garden where an old chair had been left under a cypress tree. He sat with his head in his hands.

"Do you want to tell me what is wrong?" asked Amelia.

"What is WRONG?" he shouted at her. "What is WRONG? Everything's fucking wrong. We are going back to the UK at the end of the tenancy. End of."

Did that mean the end of their relationship? Or did it just mean the end of the Cyprus 'adventure?' What exactly did he mean?

It wasn't the appropriate time to question him. He was angry and she wanted to avoid any further confrontation. She returned to the house and began to wonder the whereabouts of that letter. It was the letter wasn't it? Something contained in that little blue airmail envelope had upset Michael. She was more determined than ever to find it.

She checked that he was still sitting at the furthest end of the garden and slipped quietly into the bedroom. The clothes he had worn yesterday were slung over a wooden towel rail in the corner of the small room.

She slipped her fingers into the pockets, one by one, but apart from a linen handkerchief and the bus ticket, there was nothing.

She moved to the window to check that he was still in the same place and checked the pockets in his trousers. She removed a crumpled blue envelope. Now she knew where it was, did she have time to open it and read it.

She checked the window again and he was rubbing his fingers through his hair. She fumbled nervously and removed the official looking letter from the envelope. The address printed on the stationery was from his friend's office. His friend was a leading solicitor in town.

She scanned the letter picking just the words which stood out then checked the window again and Michael was approaching the house. She stuffed the letter back into the envelope, replaced it in the trouser pocket and began to straighten the bed as he came into the bedroom.

She knew his secret!

Michael's solicitor friend, Justin, was obviously aware of the plans Michael had made. He knew that they were eloping and knew where they were to be found. Amelia was disappointed that Michael had led her to believe that no-one else was aware of what they were doing.

Justin had written the letter asking Michael to return to sort things out properly. Brenda, Michael's wife was filing for divorce and matters had to be discussed. And, the welfare of the children was a critical matter to be resolved. Michael's foolish pride wouldn't allow him to share this information with Amelia but she now knew that things were about to get very difficult.

As the three months drew to a close, Amelia asked if they were going to renew the lease for a further period but Michael became angry and told her to pack up her clothing ready to leave. They were going to Malta! This was contrary to what he had shouted previously. She thought they were returning to the UK but didn't think it was worth bringing that up to start an argument.

Michael and his wife had purchased a property in Malta about seven years previously. The intention was to renovate it and use it as a holiday home. His objective, now, was to use it as a place to stay rather than return to England to resolve all these outstanding matters.

Amelia should have realised by then that he either had too much pride, or was a coward but she didn't think she had much choice other than to go along with his plans. Like him, she didn't have a job and had no place to return to.

Michael made all the arrangements, booked the flight giving Amelia just two days to pack and leave the villa in the state in which they had found it. They seemed to have acquired a lot of paperwork, books and food which had to be disposed of. Michael wasn't helpful but took himself to the end of the garden to sit in the shade of the sun which was becoming hotter as they approached summer.

The house didn't have air conditioning and the only fan was in the bedroom. Amelia struggled with the cleaning, her sweaty hair falling about her neck and shoulders. 'Nothing is forever,' she encouraged herself as the floor tiles dried as soon as she had wet them and her hair got wetter!

She packed both suitcases and as she folded Michael's trousers, wondered if she might have time to read the letter completely but again, he came indoors denying her the opportunity.

They had enough Cypriot Pounds (CYP) and could have afforded a taxi to Nicosia airport, but Michael's meanness came to the fore when they struggled with much heavier suitcases to the 'stop' where the local bus parked.

Being the gentleman that he believed he was, he barged up the steep steps of the old bus, suitcase before him and banged it down between the rows of seats blocking Amelia's path. He stood for a few seconds debating where they might sit. There were only six others seated randomly about the bus so he settled for a place midway. Amelia followed, her suitcase bouncing off the seats on either side of the aisle.

The driver called to them obviously asking them to pay so Michael stepped over his suitcase and fumbled in his pockets to give the correct money in exchange for a ticket which resembled that of a draw ticket.

Once seated with the baggage placed above them, they prepared for their journey back to the airport. Local ladies boarded the bus at intervals, with chickens in boxes, baskets of eggs and other outlandish things to sell at the market. Of all days they chose a market day in which to travel. The sound of the birds squawking and the high pitch of the ladies screaming got the better of Michael. As soon as they arrived in Nicosia he grabbed his suitcase and ran to the front of the bus before anyone could stand, ignoring the bus driver's good wishes for a "lucky" day.

There wasn't a bus directly to the airport so they had to get a taxi. Michael wanted to know how much it would cost before they started off but Miguel the driver only spoke two words of English so that was non-productive.

The airport was fairly quiet in contrast to the journey on the bus. They checked in and sat to wait for the flight to Luqa, Malta.

Amelia sat quietly mulling over how she had got to this point. Three months' ago she was temping for an agency, sent to a multi-national company, having a fun affair with no ties and now, she was on her way to Malta as a common law wife.

The cowbell rang! Someone was at the door! Amelia came out of her dream and met the postman who was delivering her order for glucose-free, sugar-free foodstuffs. The parcel required a signature.

"Lovely day!" smiled the postman. "Looks like it might rain later on. Oh well, that's our English weather! Have a good one!"

Amelia took the parcel and placed it on the kitchen table with the books and journals she had been writing.

'Mmmn' she thought. 'The English weather is unpredictable. If only we had summers like the ones spent in the Mediterranean.'

Michael and Amelia stepped out of Luqa airport into the humidity. Malta was very hot. It was a dry heat she supposed because the country is built on rock. That lovely honey-coloured rock which exudes a particular atmosphere of foreign-ness.

Condensation covered the inside windows of the local bus and the driver constantly wiped the windscreen with the back of his hand. Amelia hoped he was in control as there was heavy traffic about.

After thirty minutes the bus came to a halt in Zurrieq, one of the oldest towns in Malta dating back to the Bronze and Punic times. Hidden behind the huge church of St Catherine of Alexandria between the tall buildings, Michael's house was the largest in the tiny narrow street. It had five steps to the huge double front door overhung by a concrete porch heavily carved with flowers and motifs. As they mounted the steps a small woman dressed in black passed on her way to Mass.

Once inside the doors a wide passage with patterned floor tiles opened into a courtyard with lemon trees and orange trees along the boundary side.

A flight of wide concrete steps to the left of the courtyard took them up to the first floor where the living accommodation was proposed. At that time the rooms were bare. A dirty lavatory and cracked washbasin were located off the courtyard. It was very basic.

Amelia wondered how they would sleep and eat. There was no kitchen. The facilities at the villa in Kyrenia were basic enough, but this was really rudimentary.

Michael spent no time in hiring a scooter which enabled him to travel to places where he could buy hardware. He had a project. He was going to work as a carpenter, plumber and electrician. He was going to get the place habitable.

Within a short time, he had managed to persuade the local laid-back Maltese to deliver wood, concrete and bathroom equipment to the house whereupon he set to building an open-air bathroom under an archway off the courtyard.

A bed was delivered and taken up the steps to the first floor. One of the rooms was going to be a bedroom. The mattress for the bed arrived hours later so the bed was made up in readiness for their first night in Malta.

A light bulb on the end of a long flex served its purpose and was moved from room to room as required. By the light of this contraption, Amelia spied cockroaches walking along the wall. She was freaked out and leapt out of the bed, her bare feet picking up the dust from the cold tiles.

"Oh for God's sake woman, get into bed. They can't eat you alive," Michael shouted as he pulled the sheet over himself. They had only purchased pillows and a couple of sheets as the hot summer was approaching. A small fan worked overtime to keep the room cool.

Amelia couldn't bring herself to kill the creatures, besides, they were too high for her to reach. They would certainly have to buy insect killer in the morning. She couldn't bring herself to live alongside these awful trespassers.

Michael got out of bed and grabbed her by her shoulders. His large hands gripped deep into her muscles as he shook her violently.

"Get into fucking bed and stop this nonsense," he splattered as he flung her on to the hard mattress.

Was this the beginning of a catalogue of abuse?

She rolled over and pulled the sheet over her. Michael ignored her sobs, reached out and pulled the flex of the light towards him and turned the room into darkness. This was purgatory for Amelia. She would never sleep with company falling off the walls.

"Milia, Milia, Milia ….." Shouting could be heard from the Maltese woman next door. She could climb the steps leading to her roof and look down into the courtyard and see straight into their bathroom. This morning she was in her little courtyard adjacent to theirs, calling to Amelia.

"Milia, come …. Come …"

Amelia opened the large, heavy oak door leaving it ajar and walked a few steps to the small narrow door next to their house. She knocked upon it and it was immediately opened by Geyta, a young married woman with two tiny boys aged two and three years.

"Come, Milia to the inside," Geyta spoke in Pidgin English.

Amelia stepped into a dark room having no windows and heavy curtains at the end which opened up to their very small courtyard. Photographs around the room proved that it had accommodated parties at celebrations such as first communions, baptisms, marriages, and no doubt funerals.

Stepping up and under the hanging net curtain Amelia walked into the area which she called the kitchen. It was merely a room erected with breeze blocks by Lucu, her out-of-work husband. It had no kitchen function.

Geyta struck a match and lit the gas primus stove under the kettle. She had already prepared a dirty thermos with hot water for Lucu's lunch. Taking four slices of bread from the packet she placed them on the corner of the sink. With a blunt breadknife she sliced a tomato and pressed it deep into the bread soaking it. She then sprinkled each slice heavily with salt and pepper then drizzled olive oil over the pieces before patting them together and cutting them in half. From the drawer in the vegetable rack she produced a piece of crumpled paper which she smoothed with the back of her hand before tearing it and wrapping the sandwiches popping a couple of pieces of ricotta cheese into the parcel. That was Lucu's lunch taken care of.

Lucu was in his late twenties. Retired, but retired from what? During the few years they had been married he hadn't always worked. He had been a painter and decorator, a labourer and stone wall builder but mostly had kept the bed warm. He would go out drinking alone the result of which a hangover prevented him from getting up in the mornings to go to work. Geyta took several cleaning jobs to make ends meet financially. In fact it was only after having a heart murmur that she was forced to give up her work. Now, living only on a government hand-out, things were tough so the opportunity of working the odd job now and then was quite attractive for Lucu.

"Why he shout at you in the night, Milia? We hear him shouting for you. He is bad man."

Geyta opened a cupboard door to fetch out a saucer to make Amelia a 'nice cup of tea.' She reached a cup, shook it and out fell a cockroach. She rubbed the inside of the cup with her hand and promptly poured hot water into it followed by a small amount of chicory and pasteurised milk. Was this her idea of a cup of tea or coffee?

"Here," she offered. "Take … drink … make you better," she beckoned for Amelia to sit on a metal stool positioned near to the sink.

Amelia could feel herself retching. Geyta was such a kind young woman. She lived in poverty – had no kitchen as such; obtained her water from a communal tap in the street; had a make-shift lavatory in the courtyard which, when filled, was tipped on to the only bit of soil they had in the corner. Flies swarmed everywhere and the children just accepted that the flies would crawl on their faces. They didn't flinch.

Amelia thanked Geyta while she sat on the old metal chair and Geyta leaned against a wall posed to talk this out with her new neighbour.

"How he shout at you? You are beautiful," she gesticulated throwing her arms in the direction of Michael's home. "He don't shout at the other one when she come."

Amelia wasn't really listening. She was too intent on fathoming a way of disposing of her 'coffee.' There wasn't much soil and no pot plants to give it to and she was certain that she wasn't going to drink it after sharing the cup with a cockroach.

A voice could be heard calling Geyta. Someone was calling from the door so Geyta moved from her seat on the wall to see who it was. Amelia seized the opportunity to throw the drink on to the manure pile. The flies dispersed in a black cloud but it was not noticed by Geyta nor her guest, a small old lady with blackened hair, limping but propped by a hefty pine branch serving as a walking stick.

Amelia seized the appropriate moment to leave saying she had to go shopping and would call round again another time. Geyta showed her to the door, pointing out the step in the darkened room, and assuring Amelia that she should 'come to my house' if he shouts at you again!

They needed some basic furniture so Michael insisted that Amelia travelled with him to Hamrun, the town where the streets were full of furniture shops. She had to trust him by sitting pillion on the motor scooter.

She nervously mounted the machine whilst Michael steadied it. She thrust her arms tightly around his waist and closed her eyes. It wasn't exhilarating as most bragged; in fact it was terrifying and she was relieved when they came to a halt in a long street of dusty shops.

They needed a table and some chairs and a wardrobe. These pieces were selected from hundreds strewn about a dirty shop with a promise of delivery today! All the shops were similar selling similar goods and similarly dusty with sawdust flying out of the doors in the wind covering the streets. One could mistake the streets as being paved with gold!

Of course Michael needed a workbench and other tools so they trudged up and down the street searching out for these items being told by one shopkeeper, "No English." And another, "No English."

On the return journey Michael decided to do a detour and arrived at a disused airport runway. He dismounted the scooter, holding it until Amelia got off then informed her that it was her turn to have a go!

He explained how to use the throttle and change gear but Amelia was petrified. She hadn't expected this and didn't want to try to drive it. He insisted and to avoid an argument she climbed into the driver's position whilst he still held the machine upright. She managed to rev it and then took off like a rocket only to end up on the tarmac with the scooter on top of her.

Michael stood with his hands on his hips and roared with laughter. He didn't think that she might be injured or that the scooter might be damaged. After all, it was only on hire. None of these things occurred to him. He thought the whole scenario was laughable.

Amelia struggled to push the bike off her legs and stumbled to her feet. Her legs were grazed and bleeding but otherwise she was in fine form. She kicked the bike. She didn't care whether it was damaged.

There were only a few bumps and scratches on the scooter which could easily be knocked out. The journey back to the house was not enjoyable and Amelia kept her eyes closed for the duration of the trip.

The shopkeeper in Hamrun had promised delivery of the furniture that day so they left the front doors ajar just in case they didn't hear him arrive. They were still waiting at 7pm but having no telephone they were unable to find out what was happening. Had they had a phone, it was highly improbable that the shop had one so they had to leave it to chance.

Four weak looking men in their forties arrived at 10am the following morning. The truck took up all the roadway allowing only inches between some of the houses. They quickly unloaded the furniture and dumped it in the courtyard. They were about to go when Michael instructed them to take it up to the first floor. There were mumblings in Maltese and a few black looks but they did as told despite knocking a door off the wardrobe. She wondered whether it was intentional.

The sound of horns blowing in the street alerted them to a string of cars wanting to pass. The men didn't seem phased and took their time, hovering perhaps for a tip but they were not successful with Michael!

The truck moved, the cars dispersed and the street became quiet once more apart from Geyta shouting at her little boys.

Michael wanted to get his money's worth from a hire car so the building work went 'on hold' for a few days whilst they visited some of the tourist spots. Their journey to Valletta, the capital of Malta, took them to the beautiful terraced Barrakka Gardens where the delicate smell of bougainvillea likened to honeysuckle and other fragrances filled the air.

The temperature was getting warmer and as they had left Zurrieq, where the house was located, quite late in the morning, Amelia found the heat quite tiring despite being covered with a broad rimmed sunhat.

They mingled with the tourists and found a bench in the shade where they sat and watched Americans with their cameras slung around their necks and Japanese with huge camera contraptions and lenses that stretched across their chests. All were keen to photograph the Grand Harbour with boats coming in and out.

Michael suggested that they had lunch so walked within the walled city and up the steep cobbled streets until they found a small restaurant resting on the bastion walls. It was part of a very fancy hotel overlooking Marsamxett Harbour. He selected a table near to the wall with a splendid view of the boats in the harbour. His passion for sailing was resurrected as he monitored a couple taking off in their yacht. He and Amelia had enjoyed many sailing weekends on his boat in North Wales. She wondered whether he was regretting leaving that life behind.

Under the shade of a large parasol he ordered a bottle of his favourite local Marsovin wine. The waiter delivered two wine glasses and poured out the drinks, asking at the same time, if they would like to order 'the food.' He placed a basket of Maltese bread on the table with olive oil and tomato paste – tasters before the main meal.

Michael dug into the bread pouring the olive oil thickly over the soft white bread. His teeth bit into the hard, crunchy crust sending crumbs across the table. The bread was, indeed, delicious and so fresh. The bakers begin the bread making very early in the morning but it only stays fresh for a day.

The waiter reappeared carrying a dish of olives then enquired again about what food they would like to order. Michael wanted lampuka as it was in season so Amelia ordered swordfish. She was very thirsty and it was very hot seated where they were so she also ordered water. At that, Michael ordered Cisk, the local beer. She could see that with the mixture of wine, beer and sunshine that she could expect an excitable afternoon!

After lunch they rambled through the narrow streets which were quite cool, creating a vortex of warm breeze that was refreshing for Amelia. Michael stumbled over the crooked pavings. They gazed into dark shops and ogled at the Pizzarias displaying pastries to die for.

When they arrived at the car, which had been parked in a side street above the town, they noticed that it was serving as a shady rest place for seven or eight stray cats. A partly eaten fish had been left on the bonnet and birds had used the windscreen as a lavatory. None of this had been apparent to Michael inebriated as he was.

The journey back to Zurrieq was erratic with Michael cursing everyone on the road. He wove the car in and out of traffic sounding the horn as though he were a local. Amelia was relieved when they approached their narrow street behind the church in the square. There was only just enough space for another vehicle to pass once Michael had rammed the car against the wall of the house. Amelia climbed over the driver's seat to get out. Geyta heard the car door slamming and went out into the street holding a large saucepan.

"Milia! Milia! I have the lunch for you," she beckoned taking the lid off the pan to disclose the red eyes in a poor rabbit's head.

"Take some Milia for you. Some for you and some for me. I make it."

Amelia found a dish small enough to accept a token offering and with thanks said she would take it inside, thus avoiding a broken conversation in the street within Michael's hearing.

He decided to continue with his plumbing work despite his dexterity being impaired. Amelia left him to it and remembered the letter. She wondered where he may have hidden it, if, indeed it was hidden.

She looked through the pockets of his limited wardrobe but found nothing. She thought it may have been left in the suitcase and sure enough, screwed up and concealed in the lining pocket was the blue air mail letter.

Amelia wanted to read it properly. She wanted to take her time to read every line. It was as she had thought when she had scanned it before. Michael was required to return to the UK to discuss the future of his children and to agree divorce settlement terms. Why didn't he reply? Or perhaps he had! Amelia didn't know anything because he didn't discuss anything.

It would have been better if Michael had not taken to his work after their trip to Valletta as he sawed through drainage pipe in the wrong place, rendering the piece useless. The following day he suggested that they travelled to Gozo.

Amelia was agreeable, having never been to the sister island so looked forward to perhaps an adventure?

They started out early in the morning to get to the north of Malta to Cirkewwa where the ferry took passengers and vehicles over to Gozo. They made good time and were ready to queue for the short 30 minutes' boat trip after Michael had purchased the ticket from the little ticket office.

They had chosen a quiet day after the weekend when there were fewer tourists. The crossing was smooth and the blue sea calm and transparent. On arrival at Mgarr, Gozo they drove off the boat and ascended the hill towards the capital, Rabat (also called Victoria). Curious to see the little shops, they parked the car near to St George's Basilica. Amelia had heard that this was renowned for its marble and gold although they didn't inspect!

Almost every street appeared to have a church! And, almost every little shop had a statue of some religious icon. Souvenir shops displayed ornaments of the Basilica, rosaries, crucifixes and all the religious paraphernalia that one could think of.

They walked within the Citadel and wandered through the folklore museum before leaving the town to explore more of the island.

Taking a road to the south west they drove without direction until they arrived at Xlendi Bay. This was a charming quiet little place with steep cliffs on either side of the bay, sheltering it somewhat. Michael and Amelia walked alongside the water noticing women sitting in their doorways making lace with bobbins as they had done according to tradition. Not all of the women were old and Amelia stopped to chat with one young woman who had two babies at her feet whilst she needled away at a long piece of lace which she said was a collar. It was so fascinating to Amelia whose only prowess was completing a scarf in readiness for winter. It had taken her three years to finish!

After drinking Kinnie, the local orange drink, in a bar overlooking the waterfront, they continued their journey north towards Marsalforn passing little villages or hamlets on the way. Set between Xaghra and Zebbug, Marsalforn was a popular resort with the local families, both from Gozo and Malta.

They walked around the Bay passing a few bars and cafes. The small beach was quiet with only a few people with children who were making sandcastles with their newly acquired buckets and spades. Bathers lay on the rocks along each side of the bay and young lads jumped from the rocks into the deep water with no fear.

Continuing along the promenade to the head of the bay it was getting hotter so they returned to the car and decided to carry on their tour towards Ramla Bay. Described as Gozo's best beach they were curious to see what it had to offer and were not disappointed discovering how red the sand was.

Amelia kicked off her shoes and walked to the water's edge, paddling in the shallow, clear water. They had the beach to themselves but didn't have the urge for playfulness. It was too hot and Amelia was tired. She would happily have returned to Malta there and then, but they said they would 'do' the entire island.

As they gravitated south towards the harbour on the coastal road, they drove into Xwegni where the golden rocks, smooth as silk, opened up to glistening salt pans. It was truly the most magnificent sight Amelia had ever seen. A scenario that would stay with her forever.

Reluctant now to move on, despite her feelings of wanting to leave the island, she took a few more breaths of salt air and then began the short drive to Mgarr Harbour where they were just in time for the next ferry crossing to Malta.

Amelia was brought back to reality by banging noises outside. She realised that the farmer was shooting in the copse behind the apple orchard. She glanced at her watch. She had been daydreaming for at least an hour and should really ruffle her feathers and do something positive today. Yesterday had been one of her worst. She had no energy and although had managed to get dressed, very soon went back to bed. This could not be depression. She wasn't crying every second of the day. What on earth was wrong with her?

She struggled to reach her coat which was hung on the back of the door. Going out *must* change things. If only to the village shop to purchase a newspaper. That is what she would do. She would get a newspaper.

Walking was out of the question so she climbed into the Landrover and drove into the village to the community shop where two local ladies took it in turns to volunteer their services to the people of Hatfield. Emma and Gertie were in their sixties, or even seventies, and found it hard to walk around the small shop because of weak knees, obesity and very bad corns on Gertie's left foot.

Amelia opened the door and sidled across the narrow aisle to where the newspapers were usually in an untidy pile on a bottom shelf. It looked as though a farmer had been in and trodden on the only copy remaining, leaving a muddy footprint on the front page of The Western Mail.

Quite why a Welsh newspaper would be on the shelf in Hatfield, she didn't know but it was a newspaper afterall. After a short conversation with

Emma about the weather she paid the price of the paper and drove back up the lane to her little cottage.

She had left the double gates open so was able to drive in with ease yet something seemed different. The pedestrian gate at the side of her cottage was ajar and she remembered latching it before she left.

She glanced around her to see if anyone was in the garden. She owned an acre and a half of garden which had been transformed from a former paddock. A small pond had been created on the lower part of the land and sitting on a bench, staring into the water, was her gardener. Jack wasn't due to do the gardening today. What day was it? Had she forgotten again? This medical condition, whatever it was, really was playing havoc with her mind.

She called to Jack and he awoke from his dreaming and climbed the bank leaving bits of wet grass over her tarmac drive. He was in his twenties, a university drop-out who had decided that doing odd gardening jobs would make him a fortune.

"Why are you here today Jack?" questioned Amelia.

"I was in this area so thought I would come today instead of Friday," he replied.

Amelia hadn't thought of what jobs she could delegate to him and paused for a moment before telling him that he could sweep the drive and trim the bushes at the roadside. He looked bedraggled. His short dark hair was wet and stood up at the front displaying more of his ruddy face than usual. He was growing stubble perhaps intentionally and didn't hold himself upright as he normally did.

"Are you ok?" asked Amelia.

"Yes, well .... Yes, I suppose so," was his answer.

"Well if you want to talk about it," offered Amelia, "I'm here, but don't be long because I'm not a therapist and am paying you to work!"

Jack was experiencing problems with his parents. He had recently started seeing a young girl from the village and wanted her to live with him but he lived at home with his parents and they didn't approve. He sulked as he picked up the shears and stalked off through the gates on to the roadside to tidy up the bushes as requested.

Amelia felt a little sorry for him because he was autistic and didn't realise that it wasn't a good idea to live with someone after such a short time. But, then, on reflection, wasn't that exactly what she had done at that age?

Inside the Western Mail newspaper was an article about a woman who had healed herself of chronic fatigue or even M.E. (Myalgic Encephalomyelitis) through radical diet change. Amelia was extremely interested in this and tried to contact the woman for more information. It wasn't possible to make contact personally by phone but she was able to speak to a dietician who had helped the woman in question, so Amelia asked if she could have access to the diet. There was agreement over this and Amelia was promised the binder of diet facts very soon after her phone conversation.

She was determined that this was going to heal her too. If it was good for one woman, it was also good for her!

Once she had received the diet information, Amelia studied the contents of the binder, making notes of the ingredients she would need for her new regime. It was going to be tough. She would have to kiss goodbye to sugar, wheat, glucose, fruit, yeast and all processed foods for at least six months in order to give her body the rest it needed to recover from toxic overload.

Nothing was impossible. This was *it*! She knew that she was more than a conqueror and was walking in victory over this condition, the name of which she now knew!

It was her parcel of food and supplements that had been delivered earlier by her cheerful postman so she ripped open the box to reveal what would be the path to her recovery.

Large bottle of Mycopryl – middle strength to begin with
Bio Acidophilus tablets – one with breakfast and one with evening meal
Fructo – Oligosaccharides – two teaspoons a day
Enteroguard – one teaspoon in water twice a day before food

Butyric Acid Complex = one capsule three times a day with meals
Six jars of Amazake

Amelia began to doubt whether she could cope with this regime afterall. Did she even have the strength and motivation to plan her daily meals? She placed the jars back in the box, folded back the cardboard lid and sank into the armchair in the kitchen. This was all too much for her. Far too complicated. If only someone would organise it for her but there was no-one. These days she was on her own.

After a while of contemplation, she reached into the cupboard and fished through the many packets of teas. After selecting a bag from the rooibos tea box she made a cup of tea and reflected. She drew the chair closer to the woodburner which was glowing nicely. Lighting that had taken a lot of effort but she was glad that she had persevered. The cosiness and warmth of the logs burning caused her to nod off.

Amelia's relationship with Michael dissolved in the early Seventies when she returned to the UK alone and stayed with an old schoolfriend until she could pick up the pieces and begin life again. Her friend, Alice, was now married with two little children and without hesitation welcomed Amelia as any good friend would.

Not to be broken, Amelia immediately signed on with a staff agency and took some temporary work locally. A brief telephone conversation with the woman who ran the agency, secured Amelia an immediate engagement without interview and based only on the sound of her voice! She was soon able to purchase an old left-hand-drive split-screen VW which provided her with transport to get about. Old as it was, despite the cable brakes working intermittently, it served its purpose until she could afford something better. She had disposed of her pretty Mini before embarking on her experience of "common-law wife abroad!"

Her strong Irish roots would not allow her to be brought down for long and she was soon back in the swing of working. One of her temporary jobs was to help a young accountant, David, in a scaffolding company. Amelia arrived on time and walked into a prefabricated hut bursting with unfiled papers and rubbish. Horrified at the task with which she had been presented she took instructions from David, the only other person in the "office".

Two good-looking young men were stationed in the yard to load and unload the scaffolding on to lorries, but it was down to Amelia to book in and book out the equipment. The booking in was registered in a log book in blue ink and the booking out was entered in red ink.

She had been a top secretary, creaming off all the temporary executive jobs prior to her adventures with Michael, and booking scaffolding in and out was something she considered that a child could do!

David was a small, thin person with gingery coloured hair. Certainly not Amelia's type by a long way, but her flirty, jovial disposition attracted him causing him to invite her home that evening for a meal which he would cook.

He lived in a modest bungalow on the edge of the town. One would have thought that being an accountant, he would have been shrewd enough to have made a better investment. But later in life she would learn that accountants are often not risk takers!

David certainly took a risk that evening! He cooked duck and they enjoyed the meal over a bottle of cheap white wine.

His advances towards her were not quite welcome by Amelia, but she went along with it anyway ending up in his bedroom performing an act which satisfied David leaving Amelia empty. They kissed goodbye until tomorrow morning in the office!

The next day David had appointments out of the office. Once he had left and gone off site, she didn't hesitate to grab all the paperwork into a bag and took it out to the lads in the yard giving them instructions to burn it.

Mark, an Australian, over in the UK on a gap year, had eyes that didn't require a mouth to talk. Instantly Amelia was drawn into his charisma and after clearing the office of every scrap of paper, and watching the fire die down, accepted his invitation for a 'night out.'

Not wanting him to meet her at Alice's home, Amelia arranged to meet at a pub in the next town. She was quite surprised when both guys turned up. A little disappointed, she joined them for drinks and kisses and fumbles by them both later in the back of her little car.

She was, now, running wild.

The following morning, not only did she have to face Mark and Guy, but she had to face the consequences of disposing of all the company's records. Initially David walked into the office and gasped with delight. He couldn't believe the transformation. The desks were clear and had been polished. The trays were empty. He was delighted but it soon waned when he asked for a customer's details regarding a delayed transaction. There was nothing to produce! Mark revealed that they had set fire to a lot of paperwork and, as a result of that disclosure, David promptly sacked Amelia with immediate effect.

She went back to the agency asking for another placement and was given a position more suited to her abilities. She was to be Personal Assistant to the Managing Director of a Transport company further away and out of the area. The woman who ran the staff agency offered her accommodation which Amelia quickly accepted so her small number of belongings were packed and she left Alice so that she could continue her new adventure.

Mandy, who ran the agency from a small office in her home, was a woman in her forties. Worse for wear, she was unfortunately an alcoholic so Amelia's services were mostly required to run the agency rather than going out on 'placements'. However, whenever there was an important client Mandy would send Amelia on the assignment knowing that they would fall in love with her.

Amelia oozed sophistication. She dressed well in a classic fashion and in due course had traded in several cars to an upgraded Fiat 850 Sport. Her dark long hair framed her pretty face and big green eyes drew their prey by magnetism. She had a sense of humour that would out-do a comedienne. Men did fall in love with her whilst she was not liked by most women who saw her as a threat. Cushioned in a bubble of charisma brought loneliness too.

She arrived at her next assignment punctual as always and was taken to the Directors' Suite at the Transport Company. Her position was to look after the Managing Director in the way a personal assistant would be expected.

After introductions and the request to be called 'Justin' Amelia made herself familiar with his diary records and schedule of daily meetings. Justin Armitage was tall, good-looking, in his early fifties, well-spoken and polite. Perhaps he was a little shy, or unable to assess his feelings towards this fresh, bubbly new P.A.

They sat discussing his workload over coffee brought in by a little old lady whom Amelia would learn spent her day collecting cups, washing up and making tea and coffee reminiscent of the Julie Walters sketch where Julie played an old waitress.

Amelia was happy and confident that she could eat this job. Justin spent a lot of time out of the office and said he would need her to accompany him on occasions. One such occasion would be the following week when he was attending a meeting in Harrogate. This would certainly entail an over night stay. With the approval of Justin, Amelia booked two rooms at The Majestic Hotel, a delightful old building which overlooked the town but they weren't there to enjoy the sights.

Not being sure of what to pack for the overnight, Amelia folded a dress suitable for any evening occasion, together with another business suit and blouse. She knew that she was required to take notes at a couple of meetings. Being able to take verbatim shorthand notes, her skills were in demand so she felt quite confident about her work there.

Justin checked in at reception and handed a key to Amelia. She thought they were staying in adjoining rooms. As they walked towards the lift, he asked her to meet him in the foyer at 7pm in readiness for a champagne reception. Number 123 was on the opposite side of the corridor so at least the rooms were not connected.

After a shower and change of clothing, Amelia met Justin as arranged and was introduced to a number of other influential people with whom he conducted his business. After a fulfilling meal and forced conversation, she was able to be excused with a request to be in Meeting Room 2 at 9am the following morning.

Amelia half expected a knock on her hotel room at some time during the night but was pleasantly surprised that Justin hadn't made any unprofessional moves. She looked quite the part when she arrived in the meeting room that morning. Her grey suit, fresh from the laundry, and the white blouse beautifully starched. She was stunningly attractive and turned the heads of more than a few!

The day passed very quickly, and Justin drove them back that evening, leaving Amelia in the company car park where her little Fiat sports car had been left. He offered to carry her overnight bag to her car and bade her goodnight, saying that they would meet in the office the following morning.

She pondered why Justin hadn't been like all the other men who had taken advantage of her. It was movingly bothering her. She didn't understand why he wasn't interested in her. Perhaps during the two-week stint, he might make a move, but time was running out. She was only booked for another few days.

It was Friday and her last day at this assignment. Justin was in the office for the whole day, so Amelia took the opportunity to go over pending matters with him so that he was left up-to-date with events since she was leaving that afternoon.

She took her diary to his desk and moved close to him to talk over the appointments which he had for the following week. She felt the warmth of his body as she leaned forward. She wondered whether he had noticed their closeness and would he make any response? As she drew her conversation to a close, she decided to make a move towards him. She brushed his leg with her thigh. She looked at him. His eyes met hers. The magnetism *was* there but had been suppressed. He pulled her towards him and kissed her. She fell into his lap. She hadn't lost any of her appeal. She was satisfied!

On arrival at the agency which was run from Mandy Black's home, Amelia was shocked to find an unkempt woman with stains down her skirt, holding a cigarette in one hand and steadying herself by balancing with the other hand against the door frame. Mandy Black had been on the whisky so it was up to Amelia to cook the supper and see that Harry, her son, was fed and bathed before bed.

Mandy Black wanted to tell Amelia about another ''super job'' she had lined up for her next week. The racing correspondent for the Daily Mirror needed a secretary. It was a fulltime position requiring the applicant to live-in. Perhaps she was tiring of Amelia staying with them, or more to the point, she couldn't find a suitable person to fulfil the specifications of the position.

Amelia had the weekend to pack up her belongings and prepare herself for a new, permanent, job and early on Monday morning she began the journey to the country house which John Sparey rented with his common-law wife and two children from a former marriage.

The drive to the manor house was long with a circular parking area at the front. Two large pillars guarded the old oak door.

She knocked with the brass lion's head and a small, overweight fellow with pinstriped trousers opened the door. She thought at first he might be a butler, but was indeed, the boss himself!

A quick tour of the downstairs gave Amelia a bad impression. It was very dark and unfriendly. No-one else was in the property until his woman-friend came home from working in Birmingham. It was a considerable distance away and invariably she would arrive home after supper, so Amelia's job would be to cook for John Sparey and his two adult children.

Her room was at the front of the house with a large bay window overlooking the drive, shaded with large oak trees. It felt damp. The frame of a four-poster accommodated an ill-fitting mattress and two big wardrobes furnished one wall. The bathroom was at the other side of the house along a creaky highly polished wooden landing.

Amelia took the attitude that she would 'give it a try' and that it wouldn't be the end of the world if it didn't work out!

Breakfast was a family affair except that Geraldine, his partner, had already left the house at 6am to get to Birmingham. Boiled eggs were on the menu and had been cooked by John Sparey's autistic daughter, Amanda, who was twenty years old. Amanda was extremely bossy and told Amelia to turn her egg the other way in order to take it's hat off. Amelia didn't think this permanent job would be very permanent but it was early days.

John told her to get ready because they were off to Doncaster today. What was she supposed to wear? She had a very nice outfit; red skirt and top with white spots and red knee-high boots. Yes, that would do nicely! John agreed!

John Sparey was an alcoholic. He needed Amelia to drive, cook, write up his columns to a deadline, meet influential people and entertain! She felt quite capable of doing all these things if she was going to have any fun. Without fun, it wasn't going to work.

He pulled his MG sports car into the drive and then moved into the passenger seat for Amelia to take the wheel. She was a good driver and could drive anything with a steering wheel. She was fast, too.

On arrival at the course, they parked in the allotted area for the Media and were immediately escorted to the hospitality area where John handed a glass of champagne to Amelia. It would be the first of many.

Lunch was a lavish affair with smoked salmon, caviar and more champagne. Her eyes were being opened wide at the way in which these people were entertained and the lifestyles they were living - all benefits in kind.

After swigging champagne all day, Amelia actually drank herself sober and was required to drive John home. There wasn't much traffic on the roads and breathalysers hadn't been thought of! She swung the vehicle along the empty motorway reaching speeds of ninety miles an hour. John was sleeping.

Little did she realise that this was to be the format of her working days from now on. It would be Doncaster one day, Cheltenham for the duration of the event which was usually four days, Aintree, Ascot, Catterick Bridge, Chepstow, Goodwood, Ludlow, Market Rasen, Haydock, Redcar, Newmarket, York etc etc.

Wherever the destination, they were treated like royals having special seats and food and drink on tap all day.

John Sparey took great pride in introducing Amelia to his 'colleagues' as one might put it. Always inebriated, he was happy to parade her on his arm as a fashion accessory, but didn't push his attention where it would go unwanted. She was his personal assistant/driver who lived in his home with his family.

Satisfied with how things were, Amelia appeared to be settling in quite well. She had been 'working' for over a month when one night she was awakened by the sound of a creaking floor board in her room. It was dark, but she saw an image of someone standing beside her bed in a blue and white striped long shirt holding an old-fashioned candlestick with a white cloth folded over one arm, as though he or she was waiting on someone.

She wanted to scream but had frozen. No voice would come. Eventually, in what seemed an age, she was able to let out a scream which pierced the silence of the night. Amanda opened the door and burst in, dragging her lame foot behind her.

"What is it?" she asked.

"A person. A person was standing there," stuttered Amelia.

"Was it a nurse? I think it was the nurse. She attended Sir William Bragshaw when he was ill and died in this bed. She's been here before!"

Amelia stayed awake until breakfast time and was presented with a barrage of questions from John and his son, Alex, who was home from university for the weekend.

They denied that it could be anything except Amelia's imagination and when she explained that Amanda had suggested that the vision was that of a nurse, they immediately disregarded that as Amanda exaggerating.

It was enough for Amelia. She packed up her belongings, put them in her car and drove off.

Arriving at the agency once again, she recalled the whole scenario to Mandy Black who instantly agreed that she had done the right thing by leaving. She would find Amelia another job!

Another place was set at the table and over a couple of bottles of wine and brandy with coffee, Mandy set out her plans for Amelia's next placement. Only that morning she had received a call from the manager of the Manor House Hotel, about a mile away from her 'office.' He required a secretary who would oversee all other managers, that meant understanding the hierarchy of the hotel trade. Amelia was for it! Besides, it was another permanent position with accommodation. Amelia imaged that she would be given a suite on the top floor with views over the open countryside, but it didn't turn out to be quite like that.

Her accommodation was a single room in a staff block attached to the rear of the hotel. She didn't mind the noises from the kitchen as she didn't intend to live in the room. It was to be used only for sleeping.

The manager was a large, tall, dark haired fellow with black rimmed spectacles which took up most of his face. He strutted about in his pinstripes like a huge Mr Blobby. It was soon clear to Amelia why he had such a stance. Married with a wife whom nobody ever saw, and a baby, the Geordie manager lived in a beautiful apartment on the ground floor of the hotel. All their meals were freshly prepared and cooked then taken into the apartment. There was protocol here and one had to call him either by his title, 'Manager,' or by his preferred "Sir!"

Amelia didn't realise that there were so many Underling Managers. The Banqueting Manager was a tall, dark haired, handsome man in his late twenties. The Front of House Manager was a red-headed volatile, short person slightly older. His live-in girlfriend, also a red-head, worked shifts on reception. They also had a room in the hotel. Amelia wondered whether the hotel was there for the staff, or for the clients.

She soon got to grips with their methodology and learned to understand the Geordie accent which she initially mistook for Welsh! On her second day, Sir asked her to accompany him to the executive floor where the expensive suites were located. He said he wanted to check that all was well with them and it was an opportunity for Amelia to see the luxury which was on offer at the establishment.

There was more than luxury to offer when after entering the room and closing the door, he pushed her on to the bed and jumped on top of her, fumbling with his braces and undoing his pinstripes. Amelia tried to fight off the giant, and certainly resisted his moves but he continued to satisfy himself much to her disgust. He reached for a towel, mopped himself up, straightened his trousers then as though nothing had happened, continued to show Amelia the rest of the hotel.

Amelia liked to choose the men she had relationships with. She certainly didn't approve of being forced into situations like this and thereafter was keen to avoid contact with him. If he came into the office which was shared with the other managers, she walked out to reception where she was more likely to have ample coverage should he try another attempt.

Being so close to the agency, Amelia popped in to see Mandy frequently and naturally shared with her what had happened.

"I'll find you something else!" responded Mandy as she poured whisky into a teacup. Her husband, Harry, was at home and her discretion was needed as he vehemently disapproved of her drinking habit.

Amelia had changed her Fiat sports car for a Triumph Spitfire. She often left it in the staff car park at the hotel with the hood down. The car drew a lot of admiring glances, being the nicest one owned by a member of staff. She wondered whether her sophistication and rich taste was drawing unnecessary attention.

Whilst Mandy was finding the 'right' type of employment placement for her, Amelia was asked into Sir's private office suite one Monday morning to be advised that he was promoting her to Sales Executive. Amelia didn't quite consider it a promotion and was disappointed because she was not a sales person. She couldn't sell a brush to a hairdresser. At least she supposed there was a chance if one did try to sell a brush one would have it there to show a customer. How on earth does one sell an hotel?

It all became quite clear the next week when the business cards were presented to Amelia and she was told that she could use a small part of another office to make her appointments. The new secretary who took over from Amelia was Sir's sister! Nepotism at its best! Was this some kind of punishment for refusing to co-operate with Sir's sexual desires? Did his quiet wife, hidden away in the executive apartment, have an inkling of his antics? Of course Amelia was very quick to judge when she hadn't cared about Michael's wife when she was having such fun in her own affair.

The sales job wasn't going well. Amelia had resolved that she wasn't a sales person, that she couldn't sell and she wasn't going to. Instead, she left the hotel in the mornings with her hair tucked under a large brimmed hat, and drove down the lane to her mentor, Mandy. They spent the mornings opening the mail, dealing with phone calls whilst sipping whisky in tea cups. More often than not, Amelia tipped hers into a pot plant on the window sill, only for it to be filled up again pretty promptly.

Mandy would drive into the village several times a week, or several times a day depending on how her memory was functioning, to visit the butcher and take road cones and bits of hedge with her as she meandered from side to side of the lane.

"What's that noise?" she once asked Amelia as she swung the steering wheel away from a ditch.

The clanging noise they could hear was part of a road sign she had driven over and picked up which was dragging from the rear of the mini traveller. Amelia got out and tried to pull it loose but had to flag down another motorist to help, telling Mandy to sit and be quiet.

It began to rain and Mandy engaged the windscreen wipers only to find that there were none! Her son, Harry Junior, had torn them off the same day that he wee'ed in the back of the vehicle. He was totally out of control, but Mandy was never conscious enough to take proper care of him.

Amelia joined the Women's Travel Association of Gt. Britain whilst still employed at The Manor House Hotel, thinking she might 'network' and expand her skills at public relations. Their annual lunch was being held at The Dorchester Hotel in London so she arranged to spend the day in town since she was no longer 'working.'

She didn't know anyone and was seated at a large table accommodating nine others. Small talk took place between them before a speech by the President whereupon the waiters brought pre-ordered drinks to the table. Amelia hadn't pre-ordered anything. She looked amazing and must have been the youngest woman in the room.

Her dark hair was pinned in a chignon and the ruffled collar of her crisp, white blouse reached to her chin. The dark green velvet skirt and waistcoat were the same colour match as her boots. Who couldn't notice how beautiful she looked? Certainly one young waiter had noticed her and also was aware that she hadn't ordered a drink. He walked towards her with a silver tray in his hand, supporting a half-bottle of Moet which he opened and poured the champagne into a cut-glass flute for Amelia.

Heads turned. She didn't suppose that they thought she hadn't ordered it. She didn't suppose that the waiter had taken a shine to her. As she lifted the glass, she raised it to him. He smiled and winked from his station at the other side of the room.

Mandy had many acquaintances through the contacts she made in her business but she had few real friends. Amelia had met them all and wasn't surprised when she turned up at the house one day to find Graham sipping whisky with Mandy. Graham was an influential businessman in Rosedale and a director of a luxury car manufacturer. His beautiful car was parked on the drive, so Amelia knew who was visiting.

As soon as she opened the door, Mandy flew at Amelia (cup in hand) telling her that she had a new "job" for her. Graham's long-term girlfriend was a stripper and they thought that Amelia could do a strip show at their private functions which were held at premises off Broad Street in Rosedale. All the directors of Graham's company together with a handful of very close mates, gambled playing cards and drank champagne whilst being served by topless waitresses who also put on a strip show for them. Mandy thought Amelia would be perfect and, also, would earn lots of money because they tipped them very, very well.

Amelia wasn't sure. Whilst she was perhaps over-confident where her secretarial skills were concerned, she only liked doing what she knew.

Persuaded by Graham and his cup of whisky, Amelia said she would give it a try and her first induction would be the next Friday night. In the meantime, she had to decide upon a suitable bikini or similar outfit to wear. She hadn't forgotten the sewing skills she learned at school so was able to doctor a bra and pants by putting fancy fringes on them and adding a couple of stars where she thought they were needed.

The men knew that she was naive and gave her credit for that. They encouraged her by occasionally slipping fifty-pound notes into the top of her pants. She struggled with the champagne corks, but Graham quickly came to her assistance and her shaky hand didn't go unnoticed by several of the others.

At the end of the session in the early hours of the morning, Amelia slipped on her coat and quietly took the paper money from her pants. She didn't want to count it immediately but would wait until she got into the car to do that. She was stunned when she counted five hundred pounds. Five hundred pounds for a few hours' work!

After that weekend, she gave notice to leave her sales executive job.

Being realistic, she knew that she hadn't been successful at it and they knew too. She said her goodbyes and didn't bother to work the notice. She didn't need to now she knew how to make much, much more money.

The following days were spent rummaging through accessory shops, looking at fringes and sequins. Amelia traipsed from one sewing shop to another looking for tassels, pretty buttons or, indeed, anything that could make a bra and pants into a fancy costume for her waitressing. She was a dab-hand at sewing and made the simplest pair of knickers into the sexiest garment imaginable. She had collected quite a wardrobe of wild and wonderful accessories and had also become quite proficient at opening bottles of Veuve Clicquot.

She had noticed how Graham's girlfriend, Maria, was very professional at her strip act; her music specially chosen and selected to accompany her moves. When Amelia was invited to do her own show, she didn't feel she could choreograph dance moves and create an act worth watching. She declined the invitation despite lots of encouragement from her prospective audience. Her career as a topless waitress came to an end as the stripping was also part of the job. She hadn't been told this to begin with but held no regrets. Apart from the experience, it was, again, time to move on.

In the meantime, Mandy had taken matters of Amelia's future into her own hands once again and had arranged an appointment in Rosedale for Amelia to be interviewed as a masseuse. Having had no experience whatsoever, Amelia refused to take up the offer but was persuaded to just go to the interview.

Mandy took her to the suave premises in Church Road, Rosedale and waited in the car park while Amelia met the two gay men who ran the clinic. The place had an air of grandiose about it and was immaculately clean. Glass surfaces on the tables shone in the sunlight and every cushion on the sofas was plumped up and straight.

After a brief introduction she was taken into a side room off the reception area and the taller man began to undress then lay on a massage table asking Amelia to massage him indicating a few moves only to assess her touch. She did as he asked apparently passing his elementary test and was given the opportunity to work in the clinic as a masseuse. She understood that some clients would require what were described as "extras" meaning that they would like some sexual favours for which they would pay extra. She was told that other girls earned between two and three hundred pounds a day.

She certainly was attracted to the money side of the deal but was hesitant about the way in which it was earned. She discussed this with Mandy on the return journey, but Mandy was too intent on concentrating having made two mis-turns taking them miles out of their way.

She should have expected Mandy to be over-enthusiastic, encouraging her to take the place offered in the clinic. Although she wasn't 'on the books' as it were, and she didn't earn a salary, it was up to her entirely to make her money by doing the extras.

It was the topic of conversation for several days and Amelia surrendered to the call and began her first shift in the afternoon of the following Monday.

She was given white overalls to wear which gave the impression that she was a professional therapist should the police ever raid the premises. What they were offering was unlawful, so the girls had to be on their guard at all times.

Amelia sat in the reception area with two other girls. Alex was a short, rather unkempt girl with a broad Brummie accent. Her shoes were well worn and her hair was unwashed. Terry was of cleaner appearance but stank of stale cigarettes which she tried to disguise by spraying Chanel eau de toilette all over her body. They both walked outside to smoke whilst the going was quiet.

Amelia didn't understand how they could have passed the interview as the owners seemed to be so finnicky about cleanliness and appearance.

An old white-haired man walked into reception with the aid of a walking stick. He asked for Alex. He had apparently previously booked a session with her and was told to sit while Ann, the receptionist went out to find Alex. The old man eyed Amelia from top to toe and asked what her name was. She didn't realise that the girls were not using their real names and naively told him that she was who she was, Amelia.

"Oh, that's nice," he mumbled. "I'll remember that."

Amelia hoped not. She didn't fancy massaging his old, wrinkly body and certainly didn't want to give him any favours.

Before Alex appeared, another younger man walked into reception. He seemed to be in rather a hurry and hadn't pre-booked. He asked who was available and as Terry was outside smoking, chose Amelia to give his therapy.

She had been allocated a room so once he had paid his fee to Ann, he was shown to the small room at the rear of the building. The massage bed took up most of the space in the room with a shower unit located in the corner, near a blacked-out window. Part of her 'training' had advised that clients showered first before their treatment. Many didn't, preferring to shower afterwards.

Amelia looked her first client up and down. He was, actually, quite good looking and only in his late thirties, she proposed. He very quickly stripped naked and lay on his back on the couch his suntanned body evident that he took care of himself and possibly was a gym fanatic.

He asked Amelia to take off her clothes. She fumbled with the buttons on the uniform and tried to delay the procedure. He had only booked thirty minutes, so was anxious that no time was wasted.

He reached over to help her. Their lips met. He pulled her to the floor which was cold having no carpet, just a small rug near the bed. He moved the rug putting it under her and lay on top of her. She wasn't happy to have full intercourse with a stranger so told him she would improvise. By this time, he was so desperate he would have agreed to anything.

Well within his time limit, he dressed and took a leather wallet from his jacket pocket. It had a crest on the front and Amelia wondered whether he was titled aristocracy out for a bit of discreet fun. He offered six new ten-pound notes which Amelia shoved into her pocket as she showed him to the door.

"See you next time," he cheered and ran down the steps to where his red Lamborghini was parked under the conifers dividing this property from the dentist next door.

She didn't mind if she did see him again. Sixty pounds was a great amount for doing very little. She might get to enjoy this, but little did she know what was about to transpire.

Over the course of a short time, Amelia obtained a client base of regulars. She was able to choose what she would and wouldn't do for them and for those who wanted obscure favours, then the other girls were on call so to speak. They didn't appear to be fussy about what they did and discussed it quite openly between them, laughing at some of the clients who were mostly male. Females didn't usually book massages at that time in history and homosexuality was still a criminal offence. The Sexual Offences Act of 1967 was just a start as it was only partially decriminalised and convictions continued to take place for many years after.

One of her clients was Mike Appleby whose wife played a part in one of the soaps on television. He lived his life through his wife's and constantly name-dropped stars whom he had been dining with. The girls at the clinic despised him and on more than one occasion, Alex threatened to tell his wife that he was a regular.

Probably because the others disliked him, he chose Amelia every time. She didn't really like him but it was easy money. He didn't ask for much and was reasonably quick. If he booked for thirty minutes, he spent twenty-five of those recovering!

Six months passed and Amelia had earned a large sum; large enough to put a deposit on a house. Of course, Mandy had something to do with it and had schemed the whole procedure. One of her favourite clients was moving to another district, taking up a position in the North of England and needed to sell his house. Mandy jumped in with the great idea to save agents' fees and persuaded the sale and purchase of said house to Amelia.

Getting a mortgage was not an easy thing for a woman in those days but she made an appointment with a financier in the city. When she walked into his office, she could immediately tell that he was struck by her and with a little manipulation, she would squeeze anything out of him. He was like a lamb going to slaughter. She got the mortgage and the house was hers! There would be no more sleeping on sofas or being in staff quarters. She bought her own house.

Having her own front door and being able to come and go as she pleased, she decided to invite a selected few clients to her home for services rendered. This way she could charge more and they could relax with a drink in comfortable surroundings with no interruptions. Amongst the chosen ones would be the financier!

One client, called Joseph, had his own leather business and was able to leave his office whenever he wished enabling him to make frequent appointments with Amelia at home. On one such occasion, he asked if she would like to go to Belgium for the weekend. He, and another businessman, were travelling in his Rolls Royce to his friend's holiday home in De Panne. His friend, Michel, was taking his mistress and Joseph wanted to take Amelia, presumably as his mistress.

Always ready for fun, Amelia agreed and was collected from her home by Joseph in his Jaguar which was later left at a hotel car park where they transferred to Michel's Rolls Royce. Apart from some rude comments about capitalism from students driving a mini on board the ferry, the journey was short and uneventful.

The holiday home was a three-storey clapboard house near the beach. The picket fencing around the boundary was, actually on the sand.

The overnight cases were brought in and put in the dark hallway. No allocation of bedrooms at that point! First things were first and that was to open a bottle of Flemish sparkling wine. With glasses clicking a fun-filled weekend was forecast but that wasn't to be!

Joseph and Michel left Amelia in the sunlit room with Marcia, Michel's mistress of twenty years. She was Dutch but spoke very good English. She related the history of De Panne to Amelia whilst they finished off the bottle of white.

The men were ready to go to the restaurant, Le Flore, a place that Michel and Marcia frequented so as it was only a short walk away, that is what they did.

The restaurant, obviously very popular, was extremely busy and hot. A bottle each of Pinot Meunier and Reisling were ordered before the food was discussed. They all were fish eaters and requests for North Sea sole, scallops, smoked eel and lobster were taken while they drank and talked. Voices became raised as others raised theirs culminating in deafening, unwelcome sound.

An impressively old bottle of Elixir D'Anvers liqueur was brought to the table and served with coffee and, of course, Belgian chocolates. Almost unable to move from the table, Amelia was pleased to exercise a walk back to the house.

Ready to retire to bed, Amelia asked which was her room. The others looked at each other. Joseph said he would show her and took her up the wooden staircase to a large bedroom with an equally large bed covered with pretty patterned linen. Her overnight bag was placed next to his. He thought he was going to sleep with her! He thought he could bring her away for the weekend under the pretence of being his mistress! He thought he could have a freeby in other words! Amelia wasn't having any of it and demanded to sleep elsewhere. This tarnished the weekend and also the relationship between Joseph and Michel, but Amelia didn't care.

Another bedroom was made up for her and she retired to bed. As she drifted off to sleep she listened to the voices downstairs. They were not pleased, but neither was she.

The return journey was mostly silent. Joseph didn't speak to Amelia and strained conversation went on between the others. Amelia was so relieved when she opened the door to her own house closing it on yet another ''relationship.''

Joseph didn't book any further appointments with Amelia which didn't come as any surprise. He didn't appear at the clinic either.

Other 'clients' presented offers of weekends away but, having learned her lesson, Amelia took heed and politely refused.

She had just a handful of trusted men whom she saw privately at her home. All were wealthy businessmen who had free time during the day to do as they pleased. One of whom was Duncan, a small, tubby, white-haired man. Duncan drove a very nice car with a personal number plate which he blatantly parked near her home. He didn't require much in the way of services but was a lonely man who really only wanted to tell jokes whilst cracking open a bottle of wine.

Yet another married man, Duncan lived a life separate from his wife who spent most of her time in the Canary Islands with their son. The matrimonial home was a large mansion on the outskirts of Rosedale where Amelia was invited many times to simply sit and drink with him. After going to his favourite restaurant, ordering champagne and returning to his home, they often wound down the evening by sitting in the sumptuous orangery, supping brandy. Invariably Duncan would fall asleep and Amelia found her way to the bedroom allotted to her.

She liked Duncan because he wasn't demanding. She regarded him as a friend despite having met him at the clinic. He just appeared to be needy.

Needy or not, the thoughts still went through Amelia's head of how his wife must feel about him having to stay in the UK to run his business whilst she lived it up in the sun. He was resentful. It was this resentment that pushed him to lead the life of a single man. Amelia knew that Duncan had had a long relationship with an attractive blonde prior to meeting her because he poured out his regrets of buying her a car and then she didn't want to continue seeing him. He had been used. Amelia didn't want to use him. She only took what she had earned and if she had provided him with companionship for the evening, then she felt entitled to a meal.

Duncan would often appear at her home without notice. Amelia was always pleased to see him but feared that one day he might arrive when she had a client. Without upsetting him, she needed to let him know that she might not always be there and didn't want him to drive that long way for nothing. She sensed that he was hurt – rejected again. That was it. He had suffered rejection all his life and with Amelia he found acceptance.

This was a friendship, but it was becoming a little too intense for Amelia. Her shifts at the clinic had changed and she was now on duty in the evenings, so had a valid reason for not being at home until the early hours. Her meetings with Duncan became less frequent and eventually she lost touch with him. She guessed that she had been replaced!

The evening shifts at the clinic were long and busy as most men dropped in after work, or after they had been to the pub. She didn't like the types that were coming in later and some of her regulars were only available during the day. Some of the men became demanding and whilst she stuck to her principles, it caused friction amongst the other girls and eventually came to the attention of the two owners.

It was time to move on again! Amelia hadn't prepared for further work and felt it was time to go back to Mandy. She wasn't expecting what was waiting for her when she appeared at the agency.

Mandy was rather surprised to see Amelia standing on the doorstep. They were friends enough that she could have just walked into the kitchen where most of the activity went on. Amelia felt the visit was more formal as she was going to ask, once again, for work.

Despite being surprised, Mandy raised her arms and wrapped them around Amelia until she almost choked from the smell of Benson and Hedges.

"You are JUST the person I want to see!" exclaimed Mandy putting her cigarette back into the side of her mouth, gesturing for Amelia to come inside.

She pushed open the door to the small room used as an office, shuffled some papers about, moved the telephone, looked through some papers on the floor, then found what she was looking for.

"Let's go into the kitchen to talk."

Mandy had received a job vacancy from a very important client asking to interview for a top position in the Middle East. She didn't have anyone suitable on her books and knew that Amelia was just the person they would want. At least, she would make a very good interviewee and that would reflect well on the agency.

Amelia wasn't sure whether Mandy was so fed up with her that she wanted to send her away but guessed that the real reasons were personal bravado and financial.

"I'm not sure about this one," said Amelia as Mandy poured out whisky in a glass. Her husband Harry must have been away for the day. No tea cups today – or was it a special occasion?

"Oh, come on! Just go for the interview. You don't have to take the job. At least they will know that I have presentable girls on my books!" she took a swig and knocked her head back as she swallowed.

The persuading continued for over an hour when Amelia was invited to stay for lunch which consisted of thick badly cut fresh bread with lumps of butter plonked on each slice accompanied by blocks of pate. All this was washed down with a newly opened bottle of chardonnay.

Probably because of the alcohol, Amelia agreed to attend an interview. Mandy ran to the telephone to arrange it and staggered back into the room, knocking over a chair to tell Amelia that she had an appointment for the following morning.

"You can take my mink jacket," she proclaimed as she stumbled up the stairs to get the garment, "you have to look the part!"

After a lot of banging Mandy slid down the stairs holding a canvas bag on a coat hanger which contained her mink jacket.

"Here, here! Try it on!"

Amelia unzipped the cover and took out a beautiful golden mink jacket. She hesitated before putting it on. The fur was soft and smelled of Mandy's Opium perfume.

"You look *w-o-n-d-e-r-f-u-l!*" splattered Mandy.

Amelia reminded herself that she wanted fun in her life. Ok, she would do the interview. She would keep the appointment but that was all. It was just a joke. But was it?

Amelia woke early, made coffee and went through her diary setting her mind straight about the forthcoming events of the day. Her interview with two representatives of the company in the Middle East was at 10:30am at The Majestic Hotel. The largest hotel in the town it boasted all the facilities one could imagine and was quite fitting for the occasion.

So far as she knew, Amelia would be required to work in a Swedish company based in the Gulf where the sponsor was a local. One could only run a business in that country if one was sponsored by an indigenous person. Her duties would be mainly secretarial and that entailed using a telex machine regularly to communicate between Sweden and the Gulf as phone calls were extremely expensive.

She took time to dress and chose a classic two-piece suit, one which she often wore to formal events. A white starched blouse under the jacket was pinned at the top with a diamond brooch, gifted to her from her maternal grandmother.

She reached for the pièce de résistance and gently put it on over her jacket. She only needed a hat and could be misjudged for going to a wedding!

She parked her canary yellow Morgan Plus 4 in a parking space close to the entrance of the hotel and stepped out of the vehicle on to the tarmac drive. Normally she would have had the hood of the car down, but it was important that no hair was out of place this morning.

At the reception desk she asked for Mr Philips telling the large bespectacled receptionist that he was expecting her. Giving her name she took a seat at the side of the entrance to wait for this Mr Philips to greet her.

Shortly, a couple of men approached her. One was tall, thin and dark haired wearing rimless glasses and the other was a portly older fellow going bald also wearing similar spectacles. Both were very well dressed in expensive suits. Both wore highly polished leather shoes. It was obvious to Amelia that they were accustomed to wealth.

She noticed that the shorter of the two was giving her his sign of approval by shifting his eyes up and down not missing anything and particularly not missing the mink jacket.

They asked her to follow them to a suite on the first floor where a table had been laid with a crisp, white cloth upon which were coffee cups and biscuits. She was invited to sit at another table positioned at angles across the small room. The two men sat opposite shuffling papers before they addressed her.

"Well, good morning Miss Stanton. How nice to meet you. Thank you for coming this morning," smiled the taller man. "Let me introduce myself. I am Terry Johnson and my colleague and business partner here, is Gustav Larsson.

To tell you a bit about our company, I will say that we have a Swedish company based in one of the Gulf states which you may know is near the United Arab Emirates. We are close neighbours with Saudi Arabia if that means anything to you."

Amelia thought he was being patronising and told him that she was well informed and would like to know more about their company. What did they do? How many were employed? Why were they based in an Asian country?

Rather impressed with the questions that she had put forth, Gustav began to take over the conversation by explaining that they were an Import/Export company and the purpose of the interview today was to find a suitable English-speaking secretary to help them run the business.

Whereupon Amelia asked if it was necessary for her to speak Swedish. She was assured that she only needed to speak her mother tongue unless she wanted to learn Arabic!

Her duties would be purely secretarial. She would have accommodation at no expense and a car would be provided with the position. Her salary would be paid monthly to an English bank with no tax deducted. They offered a high salary and with the benefits in kind, it appeared to be a good package. However, Amelia was only there for the interview. She was fulfilling a favour for her friend, Mandy. She had to remind herself of this, as she began to get carried away with the thought of the fringe benefits of taking such a position.

"Of course, we will fly you to our offices and will give you three months' probation after which time you can return to the UK transport paid. If you decide to stay after the three months, then we will pay for you to have one month's holiday and pay for your travel also," added Terry Johnson.

Gustav went over the menial secretarial duties desired and as they had covered most topics of the vacancy, leaned over the desk towards Amelia.

"Thank you for coming today. It has been extremely nice to meet you. We will contact the agency and let you know our decision very soon," said Gustav as he reached to shake hands with Amelia. She also extended her hand to Terry and said goodbye.

She was aware of them watching her drive off in her sports car. She knew she had made an impression on them. She also thought they were weaklings and didn't hold a high impression of either of them.

Once back at Mandy's home/office, Amelia ran into the kitchen and took off the precious mink putting it carefully on the back of a chair in the dining room which was adjacent to the kitchen. Mandy ran towards her,

"How did it go? What did they say? Do you think they liked you. I'm SURE they loved you. I can't wait to hear what they said. I think I'll ring them."

"No," said Amelia. "It's too soon to ring them. It will look as though you are too anxious."

Mandy tossed her head and poured out a glass of Pinot Noir from an almost empty bottle. Harry must have been having another day away. She reached to get another glass from the cupboard and poured the last dregs into it for Amelia.

"Let's raise our glasses to ...." she smiled.

"To what?" asked Amelia. "I don't know if they are offering me anything. Besides, remember that I only went for the interview to please you. I am not taking a job if they accept me."

"Well, who cares," slurred Mandy as she gulped the glass empty and searched for the bottle opener in the kitchen drawer.

That evening when Amelia was settled in her home, watching Upstairs Downstairs on television whilst eating cheese and biscuits, the phone rang. It was Mandy. Amelia just knew that she couldn't wait and would have phoned up these guys to find out what they thought of her "best girl."

"They are delighted with you. They love you. They want you to start as soon as possible........."

"Wait! The deal was that I only went for the interview Mandy. I don't want to go and work in another country where I don't know anyone. I don't want to," retorted Amelia feeling quite cross that Mandy wanted to renege on their agreement.

"Come around tomorrow morning and we'll talk about it," snapped Mandy and the phone went dead.

She had obviously had a skin full, so Amelia thought she would sleep on it and go to see her in the morning which is what she did.

When she drove up to the house, she notice Graham's swanky car outside.

It was only eleven o'clock. He was early. She wondered what was going on.

Maria had gone to Teneriffe for a holiday, so whilst she was away Graham had a morning to spare and thought he would catch up with his old friend, Mandy. They laughed together mostly about old times and Amelia just wondered what Mandy had got up to before she married Harry. She had an inkling because Mandy had once taken her to see an old man who lived on the corner of a new estate in Tonbridge. His old house was the only one remaining since a new housing estate had been erected around it. Mandy introduced Amelia to Tom Gutteridge who had once worked for the council and probably was working when Mandy knew him.

Mandy suggested that Amelia visited him to give him a little pleasure for which she would be paid handsomely. Tom had accumulated quite an enviable bit of wealth having been a single man all his life. Amelia remembered that they made a date that she would go to see him and on the return journey Mandy gave the bombshell that Tom didn't have a penis! That was the reason for the visit – to earn cash. Apparently, Mandy was very young when she was up to her capers and was paid in Winstons, Camel or Benson and Hedges!

"Hello there!" Graham's smile was infectious. Despite his broad-mindedness, Amelia felt that he was a genuinely nice person.

The fact that Amelia had been invited to speak about her interview yesterday was forgotten whilst the whisky flowed in the tea cups much to Graham's amusement. Harry could turn up at any time and Mandy didn't want another row. He came back early the day before and she had to quickly hide the bottle and glass somewhere so chose the washing machine. Harry didn't ever have any dealings with the kitchen whatsoever, but on this occasion decided to put a dirty handkerchief straight into the washing machine. Imagine his horror when he found a bottle of whisky and an empty glass lodged in the drum!

"What a surprise to see you Graham. How are you?" asked Amelia as she pulled up a chair to the dining table.

Mandy quickly explained that Maria was away, 'And while the cat's away the mice will play!'

Amelia wasn't too sure of what Graham's intentions were and suspected that he only wanted to have a bit of entertainment, a drink and a laugh. She was right.

Mandy insisted on providing lunch whilst Graham wanted to take them all to The Majestic for lunch. Taking control as ever, they stayed and ate fresh bread door steps with cheese and crisps naturally accompanied by two bottles of Riesling.

Lunch was protracted and it was soon time to pick up Harry Junior from school. This commission was assigned to Amelia as she hadn't been participating in the alcoholic orgy. She wasn't going to be able to discuss "the interview" with any sensibility so went home after dropping the child home. Graham's glistening car was still parked in the driveway.

The phone ringing awoke Amelia. She rolled over in bed to see what time the clock showed. It was 2am. Who could this be?

"Hello?"

"Amelia! We were going to discuss the interview!"

It was Mandy – at that time in the morning. Amelia was quite cross that she should be so inconsiderate not only to ring so early in the morning, but also because the purpose of the visit yesterday was purely and simply to do that very thing. The fact that Mandy was too out-of-her-head to remember, was too bad.

"Not now Mandy. I'm trying to get to sleep. I will see you in the morning," as she put down the telephone receiver.

Quite disturbed, it took a long time for Amelia to get back to sleep consequently getting up late the following morning. Fortunately, it was Saturday and she wasn't tied to any schedules.

Still quite put out about her early morning call, Amelia was short with Mandy when the time came to discuss 'the interview.' Mandy naturally was anxious now to ascertain where she stood with regards to the acceptance of this job offer. It meant a substantial fee so obviously was keen to get Amelia to take the position.

Persuasion continued for most of the next morning. Mandy constantly pressed the advantages of a tax-free salary, free accommodation, free use of motor vehicle, a hot country, new friends ad infinitum.

Amelia wasn't having any of it. She had done her bit. She acted out the part that she had been given on Mandy's stage and the curtain had fallen so far as she was concerned but eventually Mandy ground her down and she reluctantly accepted the job on condition that it was only to fulfil the three months' probationary period and then she would be home.

The flight was long and Amelia was tired. She didn't know what she was entering into. Her fellow passenger didn't speak and she couldn't concentrate on the book she had brought to read. When the Gulf airline touched down, there was some delay in disembarkation. When she reached the door and stood on the top of the steps waiting to dismount, she thought she would be glad to reach the bottom step as the warm draft from the plane (as she thought) was blowing like a hot convector heater on her legs. Little did she realise that the heat was not coming from the plane but was blowing from the desert. This was 2am and hot! The humidity was exceptional. She would have a lot to look forward to because when it was summer, they used windscreen wipers to take away the condensation from the windscreens.

She was greeted in the arrivals by Gustav and his wife Elin. Elin was a short, attractive, blonde haired woman wearing lots of face makeup and what looked to be an expensive designer dress. A delicate cape was thrown over her shoulders being drawn to her neck by long fingers sporting vivid painted nails. 'Mmmn' thought Amelia, 'She doesn't do much work.'

Whilst Gustav was charming and gushing, Elin gave Amelia a cold look before turning away.

Gustav picked up the two suitcases and led Amelia to a large American Chevrolet Chevelle whereupon Elin quickly took her place in the front seat.

"The apartment is not ready," stated Gustav in heavily accented English, "so we put you in the hotel for now."

The young Palestian porter took both suitcases and placed them at the reception whilst Gustav confirmed the booking. Room 122 had been allocated so the porter promptly carried the baggage towards the lift beckoning for Amelia to follow. She said a brief goodnight to Gustav thanking him for greeting her. He told her to be ready for 9am when a driver would collect her and take her to the offices. Elin had no words to say.

The night was short. 9am came around very quickly. The room was hot despite having air conditioning and Amelia was restless not being able to sleep. So, being very tired, she dressed and waited for the driver to arrive.

A tall, well-built dark skinned young boy was leaning on the reception desk when she walked from the lift into the foyer. The chandeliers were glistening in the sunshine sending colours to rest upon the lavish furnishings. A water feature sent forth pink and blue water into a large glass pool in front of the desk. The opulence was breathtaking.

The boy looked up when Amelia approached the fountain and tapped her on the shoulder.

"Miss Hameeha?"

"Yes!"

"I Zekki. I take you to the office of Mister Gustav."

We walked to his vehicle, a Suzuki, parked awkwardly beside a Bentley Continental. Once inside, he put on his racing driver's identity and raced through streets, weaving in and out of traffic, putting up his fists and shouting in Arabic to other drivers. Amelia wasn't too sure that she would even get to the office.

He stopped the car at the entrance to what she supposed was a prefabricated hut. This wasn't the vision she had been given. The heat was oven-like and it was only just past nine in the morning. The sand blew against her bare legs as she walked to the door of this drab building, biting into her skin like sharp needles.

She walked directly into an open plan room where Gustav and Terry had empty desks placed next to each other. Opposite was another desk behind which a large telex machine and a Remington typewriter were positioned. She supposed that was where she was to sit.

In the far corner of the room was a smaller table where a small, plump Egyptian woman was slowly hitting the keys of an Arabic typewriter. She glanced up and smiled but continued to type at snail's pace listening to what was being said at the same time as copy typing.

Zekki was told to make coffee whilst Amelia was taken to what would be her station for the next three months at least. There was little to do on her first day but to familiarise herself with the structure of the company and to make acquaintance with Faisa, the Egyptian woman with whom she would share her duties. Faisa working on the Arabic side and Amelia working on the English.

It soon became evident that Terry and Gustav were rarely in the office and work was generated over the telephone. Faisa and Amelia were the only ones in the office, with Zekki there to run any errands.

Amelia was to have her eyes opened to the vast difference in cultures. Faisa was abrupt and impolite. Her requests were accompanied by hand gestures and she spoke to Zekki in a derogatory way which Amelia didn't like.

"Farash!" she would call to him. She didn't address him by his name, but by the Arabic for "Boy."

She would send him out to get egg omelettes for her mid morning break, telling him with a wave near her mouth, that she wanted them hot. "Chillies. Too much."

Whilst punching out a tape in preparation to send on the telex, Amelia received a telephone call from Gustav inviting her to a celebration that evening. It was the eve of Walpurgis, the last day of April and a party was being held in the ex-pat's pavilion. Zekki would take her at 7pm picking her up from the hotel at 6.45pm. There was no need to take anything.

Amelia wondered what hours Zekki worked. He seemed to be on call all the time, but she quickly learned that that was the way it was in the Middle East. He was a servant.

Zekki took Amelia back to the hotel, saying that he would return at 6.45pm to take her to the Swedish party. It was hot. She took a shower, took sight of a rat and a cockroach then relaxed on the bed for thirty minutes before changing ready for the evening celebrations. She had never heard of this festival and was curious to know if it was in any way connected with May 1st.

Zekki was prompt as his promise. A call from reception informed her that her driver was waiting in the foyer. Although it all sounded so posh, in reality, she was about to get into his dusty old car, originally white in colour but covered with golden sand.

His command of the English language was very poor, but he tried hard to make himself understood. At times it was almost impossible for Amelia to hide her laughter at the way in which he described things.

Her white dress was picking up sandy dust from the seat of his car. He changed up and down the gears as though he was racing a Lamborghini.

"Hameela, I am good driver. For three months I have this car and did you see any 'cretch' on it. Tell me, Hameela, did you see any 'cretch?'"

She thought she understood him to say that he didn't have a scratch on his car after the three months of ownership.

They arrived at the party and Terry greeted Amelia telling Zekki that he could leave now. With no thanks given, the boy left waving his arm to Amelia. Terry introduced her to Gustav's very beautiful wife whom she had already met. All those speaking a foreign language which she didn't understand seemed to be having a wonderful time except for Elin who didn't speak. She appeared to be in a bad mood and came across as being possessive and jealous.

After eating, the men moved to separate tables to drink, leaving Amelia at a table with all the women who were not drinking. She was so bored and tired. At 2am when it all came to a close, Terry drove Amelia back to the hotel, leaving Gustav and Elin to sort out their differences without further embarrassment to anyone else.

At 7.30am the following morning, Amelia was awakened by the telephone ringing. Reception were to inform her that her driver had arrived. Still in bed, of course, she gave instructions to ask him to return at 9.00am. Obviously there had been a lack of communication somehow. She later discovered that he had waited in his car outside the hotel until 9am!

Amelia was anxious to see the apartment that had been promised. An English friend of Terry's, Pat Wilesmith, had called into the office that morning and was extremely helpful in putting Amelia's mind at rest over a few anxieties, the dominant one being where she was going to live.

When she asked Pat about the apartment Pat told her that it was close by in a block but they had lost the key. After a long time of searching it was found and Pat took her to look at it. Amelia wanted to cry. There were two bathrooms where both lavatories were filled with crap which must have been there for months. The stink was unbearable and enough to knock her out. The only furniture was a table and bed. No water was laid on.

They returned to the office and Pat instructed Zekki to go and clean it all out. He cleaned only the one bathroom with a bottle of water stating that was all he had! Amelia couldn't see the move happening and was so disappointed. However, she had been checked out of the hotel on Thursday morning and that afternoon she and Pat took three blank cheques to buy stuff for the flat. They bought cups and saucers, sheets, steam iron, ironing board and a certain amount of foodstuff as at that time they didn't have a fridge.

Shopping was an awful experience. It was so hot and although most shops had air conditioning, shopping was very wearing. She noticed just how easy it was to make purchases without money. They simply opened accounts in the shops – no identification was needed! They then got the boy, Zekki, to take it all up to the apartment on the third floor. There was no lift!

Amelia had supper with Pat and her husband in their home. They were both from Manchester having worked in Bahrain before moving closer to Terry three years previously. As they already knew Terry they helped him from time to time when needed and explained that she was happy to introduce Amelia to the way things worked in that country, an offer for which Amelia was very grateful.

The couple took Amelia back to the apartment as they considered it unsafe for her to go anywhere unaccompanied. As soon as they opened the door, Amelia couldn't believe what she was seeing. The place was riddled with cockroaches. Big light brown ones with wings (she would never eat lobster again!) They were *everywhere*. The foodstuff which they had bought earlier was unidentifiable and looked like it was walking. All the creatures were at least four of five inches long, but one was absolutely enormous! Pat was quick to point out that it was two stuck together having it off!

Amelia's shrieks and cries alerted the woman next door who came out with her husband then they all went around armed with brooms and sprays attempting to kill them. It transpired that she worked for Terry in another company he ran about a mile from Amelia's new office. She was so nice, offering a bed to Amelia for the night, moving their little girl out of her bed and into theirs.

Amelia felt so strange sleeping in a foreign place with people whom she didn't know. It was all so overwhelming. She lay awake watching the patterns of light made from headlamps of vehicles on the road below. Alert and on the watch for any type of wildlife, she didn't unfortunately benefit from the loan of the bed and felt guilty for moving the little girl.

The family was going fishing early the next morning, Friday. Fridays were the muslims' holy days – their day of rest, their shabbat. Amelia had been told that she didn't need to get up as they were leaving at 5am before the sun became too hot. She could stay until Pat called round at about 10am and then they would decide how to spend their day off.

Amelia thought she would go back into her apartment next door to assess the situation and to find out if they had successfully eradicated the beasts who had become tenants. She felt brave enough to enter but found another cockroach crawling on a box which she had picked up. In panic she dropped the box remembering that it contained cups and plates. She was frightened. She trembled. These things were having such a negative effect on her and she didn't know which way to turn.

Thinking she might make up the bed, she entered the bedroom and decided that if she pulled the bed into the middle of the room, the little bastards wouldn't have much chance to get at her. As she moved the bed, it collapsed. At that very moment, Pat arrived to take her to the beach. Pat advised that it was preferable to go on a long trip (about sixty miles) with two cars if possible because there were no breakdown services available. One often saw cars abandoned on the side of the road with perhaps only a flat tyre.

Glad to get away from the apartment block, Alison put her swimming suit and a towel into a plastic bag and ran down the flights of steps as quickly as possible to avoid getting soaked from the high humidity.

The roads ran straight along the desert and all they could see was sand for miles. They passed a white Rolls Royce just abandoned, with a flat tyre.

After about an hour of driving without speed limits, seeing no other vehicles for the duration of the trip, only camels and goats who owned the road; they picked their spot on the deserted, beautiful beach. Alison was aware of her sensitivity to sunshine and spent much of the time in the cool, clear, turquoise water. She saw that her arms were becoming red so spent the rest of the day covered up.

The men had taken their boat out to sea in the hopes of bringing back fish to barbecue. They were away for the majority of the day and only returned to shore about 5.30pm. As it got dark at 6.00pm there was a rush to set up the barbecue and temporary lights.

A few "Y" shaped sticks were dug into the ground whilst Pat's husband put a straight piece of rod through the sheep's mouth and out of his backside. The animal was then hung over the embers once the fire had taken hold and got up heat. Fat could be heard sizzling on the fire as the beast began to melt.

In the meantime, bottles of wine were taken from the cool boxes and consumed at perfect temperature. The warm breeze swept across the fine dunes picking up sand on the way. It wasn't a sand storm, but called for the erection of a windbreak to protect the supper from being pebbledashed!

Someone had the forethought to bring a cassette player so music blared across the desert, into the horizon whilst the party began with dancing and drinking in the warm evening. The crimson sun was like a reflection of the fire, leaving streaks of indigo and magenta across the darkening vastness of the celestial sphere.

When every scrap of meat had been ripped off the sheep, every grain of rice had been scooped up in cupped hands and every bottle emptied it was time to pack up all the belongings, turn off the lights and head back to base. The carcass of the animal was left hanging from its crucifix, a feast for an Arabian wildcat or gazelle.

Everyone was tired but happy, singing as they travelled the long road back. The two cars drove parallel to each other. With windows down, both parties sang in harmony as they raced along the deserted narrow road hoping they wouldn't find buffaloes or camels sleeping in the centre of the road.

When they got back to Pat's apartment, Amelia was invited in to have a shower as the water still wasn't available in the company accommodation allocated to her. Whilst showering, Pat booked her into another hotel for four nights thinking that would be enough time to sort out all those outstanding issues.

The hotel room was not as opulent as the previous one, but was clean. The bed had crisp, white sheets – that was all she needed as it was so hot. The air conditioning unit struggled to keep the temperature down making choking noises every now and then. Amelia sat on the bed, propped up by the pillows, making a few entries in her journal when she heard a sound. Then a mouse ran up and over the bed. She hoped that it would be the only visitor she had that night as she jumped off the bed into the bathroom. She very gingerly inspected the loo to see if there were cockroaches, but thankfully there was nothing. When sitting on the throne, she looked up and noticed a hole in the ceiling. Of course, all sorts of things went through her mind. The Arabs had left it there to spy on her. She wouldn't be spending another penny there!

After a really good night's sleep, Amelia was collected the next morning by Zekki and taken to the office.

Zekki was keen to make conversation with Amelia and informed her that he was taking the car today because he wanted to take his T.V. to the butchers! Amelia didn't comment but giggled quietly as he began his racing circuit along the Corniche Promenade. He screeched to a halt in front of a local, causing the other driver to stop quickly to avoid going into the rear of Zekki. Amelia knew that he was dicing with death, messing around with one of the indigenous. They had their own laws and made them up as they went along so it was not unheard of for a person to be imprisoned for the most trivial thing if brought to court by an indigenous.

Amelia wound up her window and moved closer to the middle of the car. Her face obviously showed how nervous she felt.

"Hameel," Zekki laughed. "Hameeeeeel. Why you saw me with that special saw that I never saw before?"

They eventually arrived at the dilapidated office block a little later than expected. Zekki walked ahead of her ready to make an explanation but it wasn't necessary. The only other person in the office was Faiza and she was busy on the telephone talking to her husband and hardly noticed that they had arrived.

Zekki wanted to get off. He was going to spend time with his older brother.

"Today, I forget, we are going hanging."

"Hanging?" questioned Amelia.

"Yes, you know hanging? Killing the birds by shoot."

he morning passed quickly. Terry had phoned to invite her to spend lunchtime with him and his lady friend, Kitty. As Zekki was not available, Terry collected her from the office leaving Faiza to have her lunchtime there. Lunch was a long, spun out affair lasting from mid-day until 3pm.

Kitty was an extremely friendly person about mid-forties with auburn hair tied back off her plain face. She was quite small in stature, but, then, Terry was very tall so she was perhaps just average height.

She and Terry had met in the Netherlands when he was working on a project in Rotterdam several years before. Keen cyclists, they frequently returned to Holland where they had a home in the capital, Amsterdam so Amelia could expect that Terry would not be around that often.

Kitty's 'help' had prepared a selection of salads and cold meats for lunch followed by laminated pastries in the viennoiserie tradition. These had obviously been selected by Kitty. Terry opened a bottle of Cabernet Cortis, a Danish wine, and poured it into hand blown Holmegaard glasses. The lunch seemed to have a Danish theme and Amelia wondered whether they always ate traditional food rather than the local Arab dishes which were equally as delicious.

Another invitation had been offered for that evening. Gustav wanted Amelia to meet some business friends at a little party at their apartment. Amelia really liked Kitty but was having second thoughts about spending an evening in Elin's company. Perhaps she had lightened up a bit and wasn't so bitter. Like a picture from a story book, but, as with most good-looking women, Elin had all the attributes to go with it – temperamental, possessive, jealous, rude.

At 6pm Gustav arrived at the hotel and took Amelia to their apartment which was also close by. They could have walked had it not been so hot and humid.

The night was very pleasant. Their cook had served curry with a wide array of mezze or bread dips, stuffings, and side dishes such as hummus, falafel, ful, tabouleh, labaneh, and baba ghanoush.

It amazed Amelia how in a country which bans alcohol, there was such an abundance. Apparently, Terry and Gustav were members of an exclusive ex-pat club which allowed them to purchase a certain amount of wine and spirits each month. Of course, their allowance was always exceeded, but, so were all the others!

Elin wasn't present. Amelia suspected that she had taken herself to the bedroom for the night as she wouldn't have been allowed out without a chaperone.

All of the seven guests were men. They knew each other and Amelia couldn't fathom out why they would want to meet her. Was she expected to avail her secretarial services to all and sundry? She didn't ponder but was introduced to each, having a few minutes' polite conversation as she went along.

At about midnight Gustav suggested that he drove Amelia back to the hotel. Several of the guests said it was no trouble for them to take her but Amelia wasn't trusting enough to go with anyone other than Gustav.

She hopped out of the Pontiac Firebird, his second vehicle imported from the United States only the year before. Waving to him, she entered the reception of the hotel which was very busy with guests. The Arabs appeared to stay up all night and sleep in the day, particularly the wealthy sheikhs and locals.

Her room was dark and hot. The air conditioning unit had been left running but the room was still stiflingly hot. Opening the large window to the balcony would be ridiculous as she would only be letting in hot air. Not only that, the balcony was not just for her room, but was the length of the hotel serving all the other rooms too. She was a little nervous about that and spent at least fifteen minutes putting the drapes just right in case someone wanted to peep in! Little did she know how prophetic her thoughts were!

She undressed after being to the bathroom, remembering that the hole above her might be deliberately positioned to spy on her. Tucked under a single sheet for comfort more than warmth, she fell asleep. It had been a hot, tiring day and meeting people was an exhausting hobby.

At about 1.30am she heard a noise which woke her up. Two large white eyes were peering at her within inches of her face. She hadn't felt his breath. Fear shot through her body crippling her and freezing all movement including her voice.

An Arab was kneeling by her bed, just looking at her with those big white eyes; the only visible part of him that she could see other than the fact that he was wearing a white shirt. She was terrified!

Eventually her voice returned and she bellowed out a scream so loud that the invader ran, opened the door and disappeared.

Amelia pulled the sheet tightly around her body and reached for the telephone which was beside the bed. She dialled 9 for reception screaming that a man was in her room. A lot of Arab men ran to her room before the manager arrived. They were all speaking at once in Arabic and she couldn't understand what was being said. All she could do was reiterate that a man had been in her room.

In broken English one of the staff said that there was no-one that she was dreaming. This annoyed Amelia and she began to scream again. This was very disrupting, and the men tried to quieten her so that other guests would not be disturbed.

The manager and, she presumed his assistant, had a conversation in

Arabic. They knew who had broken into the room, without doubt. She knew. Her heart told her that they knew. They asked her if he 'wore the white shirt,' to which she replied in the affirmative. They then insisted that no-one had been in.

"Did he wear the white shirt?"

"Yes!"

"Oh, it was no-one!"

All of them then traipsed out of her room and left her alone. She knew that it wasn't a dream. Why wouldn't they accept that? She was beginning to experience deception at a different level. With the sheet tightly wrapped around her body, she sat in the chair for the rest of the night, waiting for someone to collect her at 7am.

When Zekki arrived, she cried. She was so upset and shocked that she could not contain her emotions. Zekki was confused. He didn't know how to react.

"Why you put the water in your eyes?" he asked. "What I do?"

"No, No!" replied Amelia as she patted him on the back. "To the office, please," she made the request trying to be assertive as all the others were towards him.

Gustav was taken aback at her recollection of the evening and talked with Terry about it. She thought that Gustav's reactions would be to take her back to his apartment but because of Elin's jealousy, it was difficult for him to offer hospitality to Amelia.

Terry said she could move out of the hotel and stay at his apartment until her own place was finished. Perhaps this would urge them to get it ready as until then it has been largely neglected.

Lunchtimes with Terry were times of eating followed by a siesta. Whilst he didn't return to the office in the afternoon, Zekki was instructed to collect her at 3pm.

In the meantime, Terry had contacted Pat and asked her to take

Amelia to the flat and let him know what needed to be done so that she could move in. Pat arrived at about 4pm and they walked over to the block, getting soaked with perspiration in that short distance.

Once inside they found the water was running from the taps and the bed was still collapsed where she had left it. It was opportune that Zekki walked in at that moment, having been instructed to help where necessary.

"Zekki, why did you leave the bed like this?" Pat asked.

"I thought you like it this way. Some people they like the blood to go to their heads ……."

It was impossible. Amelia just had to stifle a laugh.

"The furniture, it come by the hair today from Italy. I fetch it and bring it and make it for you," said Zekki rubbing his big, dark hands together. "Everything, he finished!"

However, that wasn't to be so. The furniture didn't arrive for a further two weeks and in the meantime, Amelia stayed with Terry.

Her life had changed dramatically in such a short space of time. From being a free-spirited young woman in charge of her own life, able to drive wherever she wanted, she was now on guard and not able to drive a car because women were not allowed to drive. This wasn't what they had divulged at her interview. Another deception.

At that time, a small town-centre spread out into the desert with good decent dual track roads over a large area. The locals love lights and the roads were lit everywhere for the whole night long. Palaces and sheikh's villas were smothered with lights, giving an impression from the air that the place was enormous, when, in fact, it wasn't. Being plonked right in the desert, night time brought it to life and was really like a fairy tale town.

The indigenous people were very few in number and the population of the country was mostly cosmopolitan, therefore the natives were privileged people. For instance, one oil company was obliged, as with every other company, to employ a certain number of indigenous people. At first, the employees appeared on Thursdays (they don't work on Friday) to collect their wages but the company was reluctant to pay them because they didn't turn up for work. *'But we are natives!'* so they get paid but never go to work! This was put on the statutory books!

It was difficult to weigh all this up at first. The way of life was slow. Tomorrow will do for everything. One could be shopping and waiting in a queue and a native would just walk up to the front of the queue and get attention. The sheikh's children are also allowed to drive a vehicle. It was comical to see youngsters of ten years of age driving big American cars to school, their heads hardly visible above the steering wheel. But, that was the privilege awarded to the indigenous.

The official age for others to obtain a driving licence was eighteen years, but a sixteen years old boy in the office, who was helping out as a driver during his four months' summer school holidays, took his driving test at 3am and passed. His father was a police inspector!

Whilst she stayed with Terry, her evenings were busy because he took her to meet lots of different men with whom he either did business, or, would like to do business with. She hadn't realised that having an English girl was a great benefit and was about to be used as a tool to buy contracts.

It was as though a veil had been thrown over her since being in this country. Her free-spirit had been choked. She knew that the Arabs had no regard for English girls as they had a reputation for being loose. It was beginning to dawn on her, what her purpose there was. She certainly didn't have much work to do in the office and it seemed that most of her time was out wining and dining, meeting men. Where was this leading?

Terry introduced her to a very handsome young Arab who was wearing the regalia, crisp white and laundered. A gold and diamond encrusted watch flashed as it caught the light from the chandeliers. A gold signet ring was on his little finger.

"Let me introduce you to Sheikh Abdulla. Sheikh, this is Amelia. Amelia, Sheikh Abdulla."

They shook hands. Amelia didn't speak. Terry walked away and left her with this handsome hunk. Had she been in her own country she might have given him the run around but as she was on unfamiliar ground, she trod cautiously.

He called a waiter and ordered a magnum of Moet. Surely this wasn't just for them? Surely Terry would return and perhaps bring others?

She was experienced enough to know that ploy. Get her slewed on champers and then take her to a bedroom in the hotel. Have his way and leave her a gold watch, or diamond necklace. She sipped from her Luigi Bormioli crystal flute taking care to make it last.

"So you come here from England? What do you want here?" asked Sheikh Abdulla as he pulled out a gold cigar case, selected a fine Cuban cigar and cut off the tip. Before one could say 'Jack Robinson' a waiter reached forward and lit it for him.

"I simply want the experience of living and working in a different culture," replied Amelia knowing full well that she was lying. She couldn't tell him, nor anyone else, that she was simply doing a favour for a friend.

She looked around hoping to see Terry and to catch his eye, but he was nowhere to be seen. She didn't realise that he had gone home. He had arranged the meeting with the sheikh, also doing favours but for his own procurement.

Sheikh Abdulla told her to drink because her glass was to be topped up. He was consuming his champagne as though it were water and began to get impatient with Amelia because she had hardly drunk any of hers.

He stood and in a loud voice told the waiter something in Arabic whereupon the boy picked up the bottle and glasses placing them carefully on a glass tray, beckoning to Amelia, to "come."

She didn't want to go anywhere. She looked for Terry. She guessed what was coming next!

"Come to my suite," smiled the Sheikh. "It is better. We can talk, maybe listen to some music, have food and a nice time. Come!"

"I need to see Terry!" she hesitated.

"Terry is not here. Terry has gone to his home and will not return. You are here now with me," he concluded.

Amelia felt she had been trapped. Trapped into a dangerous game. The Sheikh was a native and commanded great influence. If she refused his company, one didn't know what actions he could take. Reluctantly, but not revealing reluctance, she followed him to his personal penthouse suite which, located at the top of the thirty-storey hotel, gave unobstructed panorama of the town and surrounding desert, through the glass walls.

The suite consisted of a large sitting area equipped with classic Italian furniture, large porcelain vases containing exquisite fresh flowers and deep skin rugs. Double glass doors led into another equally sumptuously decorated room, a little smaller but surrounded by bookcases crammed with leather bound books. A huge bathroom boasted marble walls, floors and surfaces. Twin basins with obviously all gold taps or faucets as they called them.

He led her into a huge bedroom a feature of which was the enormous bed over which was a silk canopy. Matching silk covers draped over the bed on top of which were lots of co-ordinated cushions. The glass walls allowed the lights from below to dance across the room.

He touched a switch and blinds fell from above the tinted glass, dimming the room somewhat and turning on soft lights in the pelmets.

"Lets drink," he said after the tour. "We can talk. What music do you like?"

Not knowing how to answer his question, and wanting to be favourable, Amelia agreed to listen to Faiza, his favourite Arab singer. The music had a certain charm, bringing her into another culture one of mystery and curiosity.

"Dance!" he almost ordered as he placed down his glass. "Come, I will show you how to dance in the Arab way. It is very beautiful."

He took her by the hand, jerked and shook, nudging her off balance. She stumbled but didn't fall. He pulled her towards him. She knew it would be like this! Should she shake him off and wait for the consequences, or just humour him.

"Thank you! I think I will sit for a moment. I don't feel well," she feigned.

He was angry. He picked up the telephone and spoke in Arabic. Very soon afterwards, a young servant appeared to take Amelia home. But she didn't have a home. What would Terry say but more importantly, what would she say to Terry? Afterall, he had left her there.

Without another word, Amelia left the Sheikh's penthouse. She thanked him but he didn't respond. He had turned his back on her and was looking through the glass walls, probably at his empire.

It was early morning when the driver drew up at Terry's apartment block. Fortunately there was a lift which was a relief as the night was so hot.

She tapped lightly on the door. Terry opened it, wearing a light cotton dressing gown.

"Why did you leave me?" asked Amelia.

"I thought you were getting along quite well," was his answer.

"Well you were mistaken, Terry. You knew what that Sheikh wanted, didn't you? You had arranged it. Is this really what this 'job' is about?"

"No, of course not," he denied. "Let's get to sleep and we will talk about it in the morning."

Amelia wasn't happy to leave it, but as she was a guest in his home, agreed. She didn't sleep much, mulling over the real purpose of this assignment and how she could get out of it. She liked to be in control of her own life. She didn't like being manipulated, but, actually, that is what Mandy had been doing surreptitiously.

The next morning Amelia solemnly greeted Terry. He wasn't going into the office, which was expected. But, what wasn't expected was the announcement that Gustav had engaged another English girl to come from England to work for him. So, Amelia deduced that she was to be working for Terry.

Amelia had had no contact with Mandy because she didn't feel she could use the telephone to make an expensive call to England. Such was her consideration for the company, that she had no knowledge of the arrival of Mary.

Mary had been interviewed by Mandy and duly engaged by Gustav. Because of her imminent arrival, the completion of the apartment took priority. Of course, the breakdown of the relationship between Amelia and Terry didn't help with her staying in his apartment, so it was considered better that the apartment was finished.

Another bed, for Mary, and a table were extracted from the company and the furniture eventually arrived from Italy. Necessities like a fridge and freezer were delivered by a local electrical company. Zekki assembled the double bed for Amelia and did some preparatory cleaning to enable her to move in.

She didn't sleep much on the first night for fear of cockroaches crawling over her and kept on the light hoping that they only liked the darkness. She was suddenly woken up by an enormous bang which shook the building. The flat was on the top floor of a five-storey block. She ran to the balcony forgetting to look underfoot, but fortunately she didn't squash any cockroaches. From the balcony which overlooked the road she witnessed what had been a dreadful accident. She saw the body of a driver being taken out of the damaged car and placed in the back seat of another vehicle, then taken off at speed.

She was so shocked and upset at the goriness of the accident that she couldn't give her work one hundred per cent concentration. A scene like that wouldn't happen at home. Things here were so different. Still getting over the trauma of the early morning collision, she glanced through the office window at the farm below. It was really, only a square enclosure of sand with a couple of dozen sheep, one cow, some goats and three camels, but was regarded as a farm by the locals. To her consternation she found two scantily clad old men slaughtering the sheep. They were yielding big knives, slit the throats of the suspended live animals and let them drip to death. What else was she going to witness? She swallowed and began to punch out another tape to send to Sweden.

Mary was due to arrive in a week's time. Amelia's introductions had diminished probably due to bad feedback from the Sheikh. Next came the 'Asian Tummy.' She became dreadfully sick and thought she would die. A doctor was called for and took her pulse, blood pressure and temperature. He examined her appendices but there was no abdominal swelling.

The doctor was Egyptian and had his own practise next to the hotel. This was very conveniently placed as he was always on call for wealthy guests. He looked inside his bag, shuffled some boxes of tablets and then said he needed to get medicine and would be back in half an hour. True to his word he returned within the hour complete with two lots of pills, two lots of liquid medicine and two injections one which he administered into her buttocks and the other left for her to give herself the next day. Needless to say, she was too much a coward to perform that type of operation.

"What time I come tomorrow?" he asked.

This confused Amelia as she had been instructed to inject herself. If he was coming tomorrow surely he could perform the deed?

"You are the doctor. You tell me!"

"What time I come. Five o'clock. Eight o'clock?"

Amelia looked across at Pat. She was pleased that Pat had decided to stay with her. Being alone with this good-looking, full-of-himself doctor wasn't, she thought, a good idea.

"I don't want to come if you are busy ……." he said as he picked up his bag. How could she be busy when she was lying with malady as a bed mate.

He returned the following day asking, "Where you want injection? This side, this side, or in the middle?" He was obviously going to administer the second injection.

"You have to marry me before you do that!" joked Amelia not realising that the doctor would take the remark seriously.

"You want to marry me? When you marry me? This year, next year?"

"No thanks. I'm not in the market. It was a joke!"

"You don't like me? You joke at me?"

What a situation she had innocently placed herself into! She told herself that she must take greater care of how she phrases herself in future.

Whatever concoctions the doctor had given her seemed to work and although weak, she returned to work the next day feeling a little better. At lunchtime when she had returned to the apartment, she was just about to take a nap when the doorbell rang. It was the doctor.

"I come to give you injection," he smiled.

"No thanks. I am better. Recovered. I have been to work today," she shied from the door.

"I can give you any injection you want," he urged as he placed his foot in the door preventing her from closing it. There was a struggle and the only way to escape his demands, quick-thinking Amelia threw the contents of a water bottle over him. He desisted and she closed the door. What was it about these men? Did they all think they could have dominion over women or girls? She definitely would tread carefully in future, but she was already mentally planning her return to the UK.

The scene was being set for an important occasion in the town. Rothmans King Size Cigarettes staged a Car Rally and there were about fifteen entrants. There was great excitement amongst the young enthusiastic lads who brought out their cars equipped with masses of headlamps, mirrors and melodious sounding horns. There were about seven amateur rally teams, two from the UK and a couple from Germany, one from Bahrain and another from Australia.

Zekki entered his Mazda and fitted big iron bars at the front (no sump guard) but indeed they looked very grand. For what purpose they were fixed, nobody was sure, other than to look good. The cars were plastered with stickers and off they all drove into the desert to complete their course. When they eventually got back to the starting line, they were almost impossible to see being covered with sand.

All entrants were treated very well being given a splendid luncheon at the best hotel, several tee-shirts, hats and other little gifts together with thousands of cigarettes which were very cheap there anyway, not having been taxed.

Zekki completed at ninth position and was so pleased with himself. In an innocent, boyish way, he told Amelia,

"Hameela. It was very good. I am very happy. We got lost only two times and my car, it is very good. No cretches. I didn't make accident once! My friend, he have to make all the hits in his car, but I didn't make a hit!"

He wanted some kind of sponsorship from the Mazda agents and before the rally went to the manager and asked for money for the petrol. The agent told him that if he completed the rally, he would gladly display his photographs and give him the money for the petrol. Zekki wasn't satisfied with that suggestion. "OK," he told the manager. "I will make notice for my car and will put it on my car to tell every people here that Mazda is rubbish cars and I will make accident in the rally and show the peoples it is rubbish car!"

It was an experience watching all the local lads driving through the town that evening after the rally. They all thought they were on the race track. Speeding up the roads and dicing about in and out with hazard lights flashing and horns sounding. Even the police joined in the fun!

Amelia decided she wanted to learn the language so spoke only Arabic with her Egyptian colleague, Faiza, during times in the office. She was often mistaken for being Lebanese so speaking the language would be fun. She gradually accumulated a considerable vocabulary and found it fun to sit quietly listening to others and understanding what they were saying!

One day she did wonder whether her communication skills were waning, when Faiza asked her to bring some nail varnish remover to the office. Together with brush gestures over her hands, Amelia understood what she was trying to say. She wanted to 'make her nails for her husband.' The following morning Amelia presented her with the bottle of remover which Faiza immediately passed over to Zekki. She had instructed him to use it to clean the telephone.

"Why?" Amelia asked.

"One man, he used my telephone and he is very dirty. I want to clean it!" was her reply.

Amelia had wondered why the cans of Pif Paf (fly and mosquito repellent) were always empty when she needed them. She noticed Zekki squirting it liberally over the desk. He was using it to polish the desks and clean the windows!

They had their moments of fun in the office and were both prone to playing jokes. On one occasion a German came into the office from one of the neighbouring companies. Their phone lines were not working and he wanted to make a call to Germany.

The attitude of her colleagues was rubbing off on her and as he asked Amelia to get the call, she refused telling him to pick up the receiver and dial 15, thus getting the call directly. He would not do it. Neither would she. Afterall, she didn't work for him. That was precisely the perspective that the others would have taken.

He booked it himself and because the operator was rather a long time, dialled again and booked it twice. When the first call came through, Faiza took it through the switchboard and put it through to him. In seconds, he came into their office shouting,

"You got me England, not Germany!"

Faiza, sweet Faiza, sat calmly at her switchboard and replied, "OK. England, Germany, same!"

On another occasion the photocopying machine had broken down. People were coming in to use it but couldn't get it to work. They fiddled with it, walked around it, scratched their heads and asked, 'It's not good?' Naughty Amelia reacted by telling each one, 'You have broken it! Oh dear! The mechanic cannot come for one week!"

She hadn't lost that charisma she oozed before arriving in the Middle East. It was evident when a telephone operator from Cable and Wireless called at the office to do some repairs to the line. He was quite a good looking, tall, dark fellow in his early thirties. His sparkling white teeth flashed as he smiled and his dark eyes were penetrating. The work he needed to do necessitated him to crouch under Amelia's desk. She moved to talk to Faiza whilst he laboured under the table and was surprised when he called out,

"Miss. If you want telephone calls to UK you can telephone to me after 6pm and I will get for you any call you want."

The offer sounded tempting but she dared not accept any offers of that sort otherwise it would open the door for him to pester her in the office every day. It was nothing unusual for these mechanics to just drop in and ask for coffee. She didn't want to encourage him.

He didn't get a reply so continued with his problem solving, his back to Amelia. As he scrutinised the junction box, said, 'Hello!' into a spare handset. Amelia picked up her handset and pretended to be making a call. She answered each of his 'hellos' and he thought he had an incoming call. It was so funny. Faiza held her hand to her mouth to disguise her laughter. Amelia played the little game for all of ten minutes and he still didn't tumble to it.

Another nice experience was going camping. Amelia was invited by Zekki to spend Friday camping in the desert. She looked forward to this adventure after giving it a lot of thought. Afterall, she would be safe with him and his friends. Lots of boys and girls were going in two cars complete with kit and food. They pitched the tent very close to the sea and then started cooking lamb kebabs in the moonlight with the sound of the gentle waves caressing the shore under its reflection. She felt a bit tom-boyish but despite her ability to cope, the others took shifts during the night to be awake and keep guard as it could be dangerous in a lonely spot in the wilderness. A couple of soldiers in a Landrover visited a few times, asking for water and a camel called by just to look.

It was extremely warm in the morning as they woke before the sun rose. They prepared chicken for lunch by cutting it into pieces, then seasoning it with pepper, salt, cinnamon and lemon juice. It then was placed over the flames of a fire lit by two of the men.

Rice and salad were brought out of the coolers together with bottles of water. There was no alcohol at this picnic as they were all either Egyptians or Palestinians. Being in possession of alcohol was strictly unlawful. Perhaps that's why the police had been on watch.

They spent the rest of the day playing football or swimming having at least four or five miles of coastline and beach to themselves. The scorching sand burned the soles of their feet as they jumped into the warm waters to cool.

She found eating in that country fun too. Arabic people liked to eat with their fingers and before a meal would engage in a big washing ritual. Hands and faces were washed before touching any food. The same ritual stands before they pick up the Qur'an to pray. They spent a lot of time preparing and cooking, usually eating late in the evening any time between 11pm and 1am! Chicken seemed to be very popular and was boiled in rice or barbecued over charcoal. First, though, whatever the meat whether lamb, mutton, chicken or fish, it was always very highly spiced and peppered. Amelia had observed that they also eat into the bones of the chicken, something she was encouraged to do and found them soft and delicious. Another delicacy was grape leaves cooked and wrapped over like brandy snaps containing rice and minced meat and herbs.

She liked the little shops that had spits roasting chickens outside on the walkways. All looked so tempting but the down side was that she couldn't go shopping unaccompanied. Women needed to be chaperoned at all times because the Arabs didn't see many women and the ones they did see were covered up completely – even the faces except for eyes and mouths.

Zekkis' older brother Brahim asked him to invite Amelia to the Arabic wedding of his best friend. He thought it would be nice for her to experience a traditional marriage ceremony. It was held at the second nicest hotel where Amelia was required to enter the reception with the female half of a family. The men entered separately afterwards and the seating arrangements were also divided where the men were seated to the left of the ballroom and the women to the right.

They all sat at long tables and were served fruit juice whilst they waited for the action. Small gifts of almonds in silk purses were presented to all the guests. The dancing began and scantily clad belly dancers rattled bells whilst they shimmied their bellies much to the delight of the male members of the clan. The women were more interested in chatting as they moved into little groups keeping to their side of the room. Small plates were delivered to each guest bearing a tiny piece of decorated fruit cake. The whole affair was quite boring so Zekki and Brahim beckoned to Amelia to follow them as they slipped quietly downstairs to make a get-away. They went on to another wedding reception which was totally different. Modern dancing was taking place to the sound of a three-piece group. Beer and whisky were flowing washed down with chicken and rice and all sorts of lovely goodies. Some of the older men sat smoking hubble-bubble pipes whilst others did Arabic dancing in the courtyard to the tune of a whistle. Such was the merriment, that Amelia was dragged out to perform her own version of Arabic dancing. The others were clapping and egging her on. This was more like it. This was more her idea of fun. The evening ended with a very old man dancing with a glass of beer on his head!

They hadn't driven very far when Zekki realised they had a puncture in the car. He pulled it over to the side of the road and they all got out. He had no equipment to change a wheel. It was way after midnight so they were guarded, not knowing who might stop to help. They waited patiently in the warm air until a kindly Arab stopped. Once inside his car, Brahim noticed that quite without embarrassment, he moved the mirror so that he could see Amelia. Brahim was intelligent enough to get him to take them back to the party rather than take any of us home. It wasn't safe for their residences to be revealed to any stranger, particularly as he had taken a fancy to Amelia.

An important Frenchman was visiting Terry hoping that they could do a very lucrative business deal. Amelia was not invited to entertain; since her meeting with the sheikh she had been excluded from such dalliances. Instead, Terry and Gustav took Mary along for an evening at the best hotel in town. Mary had only arrived that afternoon so she would be introduced to the real object of her placement.

Messieur Beachene was due to leave for France the following morning and Zekki had been appointed to take him to the airport. When they arrived at the airport, Beachene thought that Zekki was his personal driver and asked him to wait.

"I cannot wait," replied Zekki. "I have my business to do. I am very busy. It is my car and I bring you. You are welcome. You can come in my car but you come now. I cannot wait. If you do not come now, you can come from the inside of your legs!"

What he meant was, 'you can walk!'

Summer was fast approaching and the days were getting hotter. Most of the population left the country to go to the Lebanon, Cairo or UK for the three months duration because the temperatures soared sometimes up to 50 degrees Centigrade.

Zekki was preparing to go to Cairo where his family lived. His belongings had been thrown into the back of his car. He came to the office to say farewell to Amelia. He didn't realise at that point that it would be the last time he would see her.

Shortly after his departure, Amelia was informed that she had been awarded her local driving licence. This would enable her to take the company car which had been promised as part of her employment package. It was strange looking at the small document which was written in Arabic and could mean anything as she didn't understand the Arabic script.

The promise of the car didn't materialise, but she was given access to the pool car which happened to be a Subaru. It was shared with all and sundry. Whoever needed it, used it. When Amelia asked to use it, something went wrong with it. On the first occasion she was honoured to use it, it wouldn't start. Another time it had a puncture. It was considered to be unlucky because it was green in colour. She wasn't amused and asked when she might be given her own car, but 'inshalla, inshalla' was as far as it went.

Mary moved into the apartment and immediately complained about the single bed with which she had been provided. Amelia had her suspicions that Mary might find herself in trouble and gave her some advice about how different things were in this country. Mary wasn't interested. She thought Amelia was over cautious and unworldly. She scoffed when Amelia warned her about going out in short dresses. Amelia had adhered to local tradition by wearing long cotton garments with sleeves and high necklines. She also discovered how cool it was to wear such clothing. Mary walked about with bare legs, miniskirts and low sleeveless tops.

It wasn't long before chauffeur driven limousines were calling for Mary. Every evening she was out. She didn't eat in the home, despite Amelia making healthy pasta dishes and salads. She was having none of it. Mary was a good-time girl, in it for all she could get.

Amelia was upset when she found Mary wearing her underwear. Mary had the attitude that anything was there available for her.

After a night when Mary failed to come home, at lunchtime Amelia noticed a gold Rolex watch and diamond ear rings on the cabinet in the bathroom. That confirmed Amelia's suspicions. She was by no means jealous in any way. She had, herself, earned lots of money from stripping, massaging and escorting but had drawn the line at certain extremities. Mary was overstepping those and wouldn't listen. They were in a country where the indigenous were above the law. She could be kidnapped, imprisoned – anything could happen if she were to upset one of them.

This decided Amelia's fate. As the three months' probation period drew near, she approached Terry and told him that she would not return once she was in UK. Terry had half-expected that news and they agreed a mutual date for her to leave.

In the meantime, she had been approached by an acquaintance who told her that a member of the Royal Family was looking for an English-speaking secretary/personal assistant. Would she like to apply? She had good references. She thought about it. She liked the country. It gave her something, but she couldn't think what it was. Maybe it was because it was so different from anything or anywhere she had ever been before.

She met the Royal and was very impressed with his offer. She would have her own office suite within the Women's Palace. This palace was occupied by his wives and their staff. Her own 'farash' (boy) would be on duty to fulfil all her needs. She would be collected by royal vehicle each morning, but would not be provided with accommodation. This, she would have to seek.

She had a long talk with Frederik who had recommended the position to her. He was absolutely sure that she would be offered the position and would enjoy it. It would be a million miles away from the conditions she had found herself in during this probationary period with Terry and Gustav.

She accepted the position and returned to check on her home; to check on her tenant and also to talk it over with Mandy. This time the decision had been hers. She was to pave her own pathway and make it what she wanted without the interference of anyone else!

She had packed lots of long, white cotton dresses – with sleeves of course! This season would be hotter than she had experienced before but she was looking forward to a new life hoping that she could make it as permanent as she wanted.

As she disembarked the Gulf Air 747, she noticed a large black limousine waiting on the tarmac, flying a flag on the front of the bonnet. She didn't pay any more attention to that until she took her last step and trod on the runway. Two policemen dressed in loose white linen garments stepped in front of her and ushered her into the waiting vehicle. Quite astonished, she wondered whether she was being kidnapped but was quickly informed that they were secret police who worked exclusively for Sheikh Abdulla. She was quickly concluding that every Sheikh was called 'Abdulla!'

A short drive along the Corniche, with which she was familiar, and out into the sandy landscape brought them to the Ladies' Palace. Within high walls, the building appeared to be huge. Lit up with thousands of lights, it certainly looked like a fairy-tale palace.

She was ushered into a part of the building close to a clocktower. These would be her quarters. Her office was set at the end of a long corridor with large windows facing an open courtyard with grass beyond. Water sprays were keeping the grass alive and were on constantly. After familiarising herself with the office layout, she was allowed to leave only to commence her duties the following morning.

The royal car arrived to take Amelia to her lodgings. The position she had taken did not provide accommodation and it had been her responsibility to organise before arriving. It had been difficult as she had relied on Zekki to find something for her, but also to keep it confidential. She was to learn about trust.

She had sent a coded fax to Zekki so he knew when she was arriving. He would meet her at the Girls' International School so that is where the limousine was instructed to leave her.

The farash (boy) who was employed to work for Amelia, accompanied her in the chauffeur-driven vehicle and helped her with the few bits of luggage she had brought. He looked a bit nonplussed and as instructed left the bags on the footpath. Amelia dismissed him and stood waiting for Zekki.

Feeling quite vulnerable, she looked at her watch several times. She was on time. Had he forgotten? She had no means of contacting him and could only hope that he would arrive as promised.

After what seemed hours, a dusty black Mazda spun on the sandy road and screeched to a halt in front of Amelia kicking up a dust cloud. She stepped back and noticed that it was Zekki.

"You have a different car!" she exclaimed as he picked up her bags and put them into the boot.

"Hameel. Sorry for the late. My car is in bad habit. The red light it comes on in the morning because it is sleeping in the night."

Not being able to make head nor tail of what he was trying to explain, Amelia was just glad that he had arrived and anticipated where she would be staying.

She jumped into his new, used car, sped through the streets until they came to a dead end in a back street. The buildings had no windows and were situated behind high walls, access being through what she would describe as double garage doors.

Zekki told her to wait while he entered the doors of a shabby looking place that looked like a storage unit. She waited in the heat. He left the engine running but the air conditioner didn't appear to be working. When he returned she asked him to turn it on and he shook his head, put his hands to his eyes and said,

"Hameel. I tell you already. The car is in bad habit."

She took that to mean that it didn't work.

Anxious to get settled in her new home, she asked if they could go in. Zekki then had some explaining to do. He had failed to find her anywhere to live during the time she had been in the UK and as a last resort, had asked a friend a favour to allow Amelia to stay there until he could find her somewhere else.

Amelia wasn't very pleased. She was going to have to stay in a stranger's home, not knowing how he would treat her. Would she be safe? She shouted at Zekki displaying her disappointment but wasn't sure that he fully understood anyway.

She was introduced to the very tall, young man who was staying in this apartment which actually belonged to his brother who was away on 'business.' He made her feel welcome and as Zekki departed offered to cook a meal for her.

Al appeared to be good at cooking. He washed and prepared lamb then rolled it in spices after soaking it in freshly squeezed lemon juice. Together with a large pot of cooked rice, he took the lamb out on to a small balcony where the meat was placed on a barbecue. He pulled up two chairs and they sat whilst the spit turned the lamb, cooking it to perfection. When Al served it, he pulled handsful of coriander from a big fresh bunch which hung from the door and ripped it over the meat and rice. It was delicious.

Of course, there was no wine to drink as Al was a Muslim in an Arab country where it was forbidden. They raised their glasses of cold water with large slices of lemon floating on cubes of ice. Amelia was happy to comply and enjoyed the company as they sat overlooking what might have been described in the homeland as slums. The cool breeze was welcoming after the humidity of the day and the temperatures of 48C.

As darkness fell, so everywhere became lit up with lights attached to the buildings, connected into hundreds of tangled wires. The moon was bright and the stars glittered. This was her first taste of pure independence, well, almost. She was depending on Zekki to find her an apartment, or similar, of her own. She would easily be able to afford to rent something nice as she was about to earn a very high salary, tax free!

Amelia was unused to staying up all night, as the custom appeared to be in hot countries and asked to be shown where she could sleep. She was very surprised to discover that there was only one double bed and hoped that she wasn't expected to share it.

Al noticed her disappointment and offered to sleep on the sofa so that she could have the bed. That was alright for one night, but this wouldn't be satisfactory for any length of time. Zekki must find her somewhere else.

She took her belongings to the bathroom to prepare for sleep and was surprised to find that there was no lavatory! A hole in the tiled floor exposed a black tunnel which probably went into the street for all she knew. The shower was a hosepipe hung on a clothes hanger over the door of a make-shift cubicle next to a washing machine with exposed wires poked into a power point with a screwdriver. She had seen this done before and wondered if this was the way everyone plugged in their electrical equipment if it didn't have an earth wire.

She looked around for toilet tissue but didn't see any. A small tap was positioned at floor level next to the hole and an empty Evian water bottle lay next to it. The bathroom was in such contrast to the sitting room which was furnished with ornate Italian furniture and beautiful large mirrors. She couldn't stay here. She would not be able to wash properly. No! She *had* to find other accommodation.

The sounds of dogs barking throughout the night kept Amelia awake. Consequently, in the morning she was extremely tired and hot.

Al was already in the bathroom at 5am. She knew that the town became alive very early and closed down for three hours at mid-day, then almost everywhere remained open practically all night. She had seen people shopping past midnight so their activities were centred around the heat of the day and the cool of the evening.

She waited for him to appear before entering the bathroom to merely wash her face and brush her teeth. Glad that she had remembered to bring her own towel, she rubbed down her body as she had once been told the Germans do instead of bathing. In the meantime, Al was preparing coffee and pastries for breakfast.

"I am going to my work," explained Al, "and will leave you the key so that you can come to the house and enter if I am not here."

Amelia thanked him and took a big, very old-fashioned looking key from his large hand. She loved men's hands if they had nicely shaped nails and Al's certainly did. They were very clean and almost unused looking! She loved nice teeth too – and he had a fine set of pearly white ones. He was nice. And, he was trying to be a good host.

She hoped that she wouldn't need the key. She wanted to leave as soon as possible. How could she make contact with Zekki?

Once Al had left the house, she smartened herself and put on some makeup. Very little was required because the heat only melted it. She locked the door at the appointed time and walked down the steep flight of concrete steps to the "garage door." A limousine with flag flying was waiting for her. It must have looked so out of place in the small back street and that could explain why people were coming out of their shuttered homes to see what was going on! She wondered how the driver had been given directions to this outlandish address. Afterall, she had been left at the school the previous day. She had no conception that she was being monitored. She had now been given access to the royal household and security was paramount, yet she was no threat.

She entered her office to be greeted by Sheikh Abdulla himself. He politely stretched out his cool, soft hand and shook hers with a gentleness which she would expect from a woman. His tall stature towered over her as he beckoned for her to sit on an ornate Italianate style chair. He was extremely well groomed; his black beard and moustache resembled a work of art painted upon his tanned skin.

"Welcome Miss Amelia! My assistant, Abrahim, will help you with anything you need to know. Have a good day!" he then disappeared with a guard following closely behind.

Abrahim was a short Egyptian boy. It was difficult to ascertain his age as the youngsters often looked much older than they were. He rang a bell located at the front of a large wooden bureau-type desk, gesticulating to an even smaller Indian boy who nodded and disappeared only to reappear moments later bearing a silver tray upon which were fine china tea cups and a teapot.

The boy, who remained nameless, poured out thick black tea into the delicate cups then left the room after nodding to them once more.

Abrahim and Amelia sipped the bitter tea while he described the routine of the office which, to Amelia, was very rudimentary. She wondered what she would do all day with so little required of her.

After tea, Abrahim left the office explaining that should she need anything, her 'boy' would come if she rang the bell. Amelia thanked him and began to look through the filing cabinet which had been placed strategically between two large marble pillars. Apart from a few files containing drawings of the garden layout, there didn't appear to be much else.

A golden telephone handset was set on her desk. She didn't have anyone to call so supposed it was purely for incoming calls. She needed a diary. She would make a list of items needed and then present it to the 'boy.'

The room was nicely furnished with Italian furniture. A sofa was placed under the large windows which were shuttered to keep out the sunlight. Air conditioning kept a cool temperature. Amelia was very satisfied.

The morning passed quickly and soon the 'boy' came to inform Amelia that her car was waiting. She hadn't thought about the lunchtime siesta and where she would take it. She had no option but to return to Al's brother's apartment, to the amusement of the nosy neighbours.

Al had not returned since Amelia left that morning so she thought she would tidy up a bit, but when it got to the bathroom she absolutely gave in. She had been given a beautiful marble bathroom next to her office with a proper lavatory although no tissue. Perhaps she would try to use the one at the palace for washing. She would see.

Amelia couldn't sleep. Her time clock hadn't been reset and she wasn't sure whether Al might return at lunchtime. She hadn't seen Zekki. Relaxing didn't come easily and soon it was time for her to return to the palace.

The afternoon brought unforeseen activities as men in uniforms descended to install a water fountain in the corner of the office. As the floors were concrete, pipes were laid on top from the adjacent bathroom. It was all so unsightly, but that was how things were done! Once installed, the water trickled down fake bricks into a bucket. Quite why it was thought she needed that accessory, she didn't know. Whilst all this was going on, the bathroom access was restricted!

Abrahim spoke quietly to Amelia, as though international secrets were being spilled.

"The princess wishes to purchase some jewellery so you need to go to the jewellers to bring it for her. You will have body guards, so it's okay."

This was a new kind of assignment for Amelia! Perhaps the job was going to be interesting afterall.

At 6pm two secret police arrived to escort her to the waiting limousine. They drove into the town and parked outside the best jeweller – no gold souq's for the princess! The chauffeur pressed the horn and out skuttled two assistants bearing boxes covered with black velvet cloth. One of the policemen opened the rear door allowing them to present the boxes to Amelia. The door was quickly closed and the car returned to the palace. It was all over in a flash!

Amelia didn't see the contents of the boxes as they were taken by the policemen to the princesses suite at the far end of the palace but she was told that the value of the items was in excess of one million US dollars!

The princess would ponder over them and eventually choose what she liked, returning the rest to the shop.

Amelia began to understand how trust worked. The minions trusted the lords, but generally, no-one else could be trusted for their word. Crime was non-existent.

She hadn't seen, nor heard, from Zekki and couldn't understand why there had been no contact. Had something happened to him? In the meantime, her friendship with Al was warming.

After the hottest day yet, she arrived at the apartment. The office had been cool, but once outside the heat was unbearable. She put the key in the door, but it was already unlocked. Al had just showered and had only a towel around his waist. Amelia would have given anything to have a shower, but resisted, not putting any temptation in the way. She, afterall, preferred to choose her men.

To her surprise, Al produced a bottle of red wine. As he opened the bottle with a penknife, it was somewhat corked, but she didn't think he realised finesse.

Two fine crystal glasses were placed on the ornate book table and he proceeded to pour out wine until they were almost brimming over. Amelia didn't react. This was a different culture. The fine china, glassware and furniture (and cars) were their most influential possessions; yet today, Amelia was asked to prepare the banqueting hall for a function and laughed at the plastic flowers and tubs of margarine which had been placed on the paste tables. All covered over with linen table cloths!

Sheikh Abdulla honoured them with his presence, to oversee the tables and commanded the farash, "Where is the Tomato Sauce?"

The boy scuttled away to reappear with a trolley of bottles of 'Daddies Sauce' and 'Tomato Ketchup' which were strategically placed along the tables. It was explained to Amelia, that the Queen of England, she like the sauce!

Al opened a large packet of crisp-like snacks and poured them into a fruit bowl. He picked up his glass, being careful not to spill any of the wine, and raised it to Amelia.

"For good friendships!" he smiled and dug into a handful of crisps.

Amelia wondered how long this could go on for. She really must find somewhere to live and brought up the subject as she sipped the warm red wine.

Al was apparently very influential amongst the sheikhs and promised that he would speak with his friend and find somewhere for her. Relieved, she finished off the wine, later finding out that an Englishman had given the bottle to Al as a thank you for 'fixing' something for him with the government!

The old air conditioning unit rattled away disturbing the peace and not quite managing to keep the room cool. The heat and the wine caused Amelia to feel sleepy. The night was young and Al had plans to go out. That usually entailed driving up and down the Corniche, having races with others, skidding and blowing horns until the early hours. Amelia wasn't up for that and chose to stay in the apartment.

Al returned in the early hours. After using the bathroom, he crept into the bed beside Amelia who was fast asleep. Very soon his arm was around her body. Still sleeping she responded and moved towards him. Their lips engaged. It was a night of lust.

Al announced one morning that his brother was returning and Amelia would have to leave. Not to leave her high-and-dry, he promised he would find a place for her to stay and that evening Amelia was not let down, as in the past. He took her out of the town to a sandy, almost desert-like township and pulled up his car outside a barn door. Producing a huge rusty key, he unlocked the door and invited her into the 'house' he had rented for her. But, because it was slap-bang in the middle of the Arab quarter, he decided to share it with her, for her protection.

Amelia really didn't have any choice. The kitchen was basic – a tap and a bowl. The lavatory was simply a hole the floor. A mattress lay on the floor. She had seen 'basic' before, but certainly not as 'basic' as this!

They took up occupancy the following day greeted by the local ladies all talking at once. Al spoke with them, giving them reassurance that Amelia was his wife, telling her not to speak! She also had to arrange for her driver to collect her and drop her at an appointed spot where Al would leave her and pick her up – all to avoid gossip. It was unlawful at that time for couples to cohabit.

Was this history repeating itself? She was play-acting another wifey role! It was fanciful!

Fortunately, this was short-lived and within a few weeks she was able to rent a lovely apartment overlooking the Souq. It was noisy, but, in some respects that was comforting. It was clean, spacious, cool and well furnished. She needed very little, had a prestigious address suited with her eminent occupation and finished her relationship with Al quite amicably.

Sheikh Abdulla very rarely made attendance in the office and sent audio tapes over for her to type out. She had the latest IBM golfball electric typewriter to make her workload easier. The work was easy and soon finished, allowing her time to accomplish her personal affairs.

Sheikh Abdulla's handsome twenty-five years old son, Tareef, began to make regular visits to Amelia in her office. He was curious to hear about England and although had only visited London, was interested to hear about Amelia's part of the world. A tall, tanned fellow with black hair and facial hair, he was indeed very good-looking. His soft pale hands were what attracted Amelia, only after noticing his dazzling white perfect teeth. Both attributes she loved! His deep voice reminded her of Leonard Cohen! Where would this go?

His presence in the office became so systematic, that a magnetism drew them closer. The young Sheikh invited her to take dinner with him at his favourite hotel, later to watch beautiful girls belly dancing. Without hesitation she accepted and wondered what she should wear. Afterall, he was a sheikh and would require her to cover up. She had brought a long white dress, which rather looked like a sheet, but with a nice pearl necklace and matching bracelet, she looked quite stunning.

The royal limousine arrived at her new apartment; the chauffeur was told to remain in his seat while Tareef jumped out of the vehicle to help Amelia.

Once inside the limousine, she was overwhelmed by the perfume which he had lavished over his body. This was quite normal for men to soak themselves in expensive scents. He leaned forward and opened a cocktail cabinet which revealed a set of cut crystal glasses. From a compartment next to it, he produced a bottle of Veuve Cliquot, opened it and poured the nectar into two glasses. She only had time to feel the bubbles tickling her nose before they arrived at their venue. She couldn't help thinking 'What a waste!' but would learn that lavishness was the way of life for these opulents! Afterall, the no-alcohol rules were not applicable in his case!

They were escorted by a smart waiter to Sheikh Tareef's personal table. Another bottle of champagne arrived, together with spiced king prawns for nibbles. Expensive, fine ruby red wine followed. The dancing began and as the beautiful girls rolled their bellies in tune to the traditional Arabic musical ensemble known as Takht consisting of four instruments; Oud, Nay, Qanun and violin, and one main percussion instrument (riq) Tareef showed his appreciation by clapping his hands together in time to the rythym.

They appeared to be dancing for Tareef and this was confirmed to Amelia when he stuffed one hundred-dollar notes into the tops of their grass skirts. Was this déjà vu? Amelia had done this very thing prior to working in the Middle East!

History was, indeed, repeating itself!

The evening continued into the early hours. Amelia was very tired and the effects of the champagne were contributing to her tiredness. She didn't want Tareef to know that she didn't have the stamina to see through the date.

At almost 3am he called his waiter to speak to him quietly. Amelia would not have understood anyway but realised he had been calling his driver. She was relieved that they were at last leaving.

The beautiful limousine waited outside the hotel, flag still flying with armed secret police in another vehicle parked behind. This was not the vehicle used to transport her to and from the office. It was a much grander beast. Telling the driver to move, Tareef put his arm around Amelia and began to stroke her back gently as he kissed her cheek. His hands pushed back her dark hair as he nibbled on her ear. This wasn't going to end in the car, for sure!

His palace looked like a museum as they approached the floodlit building. They entered through enormous arched doors, opened by a young Indian servant. Tareef ordered coffee as they retired to a sumptuously furnished drawing room. The high walls were covered with pale green fabric which matched the long curtains. Four crystal chandeliers lit the room but were dimmed by Tareef as he pulled Amelia into the soft green leather sofa. Oriental plants were placed in large jardinières on either side of the marble fireplace above which was an ornate mirror. Glass book tables stood in front of the sofas on which were French magazines and glass ashtrays.

Tareef lit up a Cuban cigar shaking the red phosphorus stick until it died. Amelia did not smoke and found it constraining.

Turkish coffee arrived with sweet almond tarts in a small china dish. This was early morning and Amelia would normally be thinking of drinking coffee with a dish of cornflakes!

He placed the cigar in the ashtray, took a swig of the coffee emptying the tiny cup and then leaned over towards Amelia pulling her down into the soft cushions. His beautiful soft hands wandered across her stomach and pulled up her long dress. She hadn't lost her magnetism but knew that this was quite different. The culture disrespected women and he was only getting his way with her. She knew that it wasn't anything more.

They made love until daylight. She composed herself making the disarray of her clothing more orderly hoping that the servants wouldn't guess what they had been doing, but on reflection, perhaps this was a normal occurrence and they were well used to it!

Tareef arrived in her office later that morning asking if she would see him again that evening. Could she refuse? She did like him. Of course, she agreed and this became a regular arrangement.

Her previous appointment with Terry and Gustav had made provision for the use of a company vehicle. She missed being able to drive and had hinted several times to Tareef that she would like to drive. Of course it was out of the question. She had her own chauffeur-driven limousine which was available to take her shopping, or anywhere she wanted. This wasn't what she wanted. She found her freedom curtailed. She enjoyed everything else. It was certainly so much better than her first experience in the country.

One evening Tareef arrived at her apartment driving his own bright red Lamborghini. They drove up and down the Corniche with all the other commoners, Tareef cutting up everyone and anything in his path.

A black Ford Mustang, driven by another native decided to race them. He clipped the side of the Lamborghini forcing Tareef to lose control at

80mph. The car veered over to the other carriageway, turning over and landing on top of the barrier smashing the flower containers and throwing flowers all over both carriageways.

The personal police officers stopped the traffic and ran to get them out of the smouldering wreck. Shocked and slightly concussed Amelia found herself being taken to the Ladies Hospital where she was examined by a female Indian doctor.

"Everything appears to be alright," smiled the doctor as she felt around Amelia's stomach. "The baby is fine!"

The baby!

"Are you sure?" asked Amelia meaning are you sure that I am pregnant, but the doctor mistook her question thinking she was enquiring about the state of the baby.

"Absolutely sure," said the doctor as she put Amelia's hand to her stomach. "Feel! It's here!"

If Sheikh Abdulla knew that his son was having a relationship with his English Secretary/PA he would not have been pleased. All cloak-and-dagger, Tareef arranged for a woman to go to the hospital to take Amelia back to her apartment once she had been given the all-clear.

Tareef sustained just a few cuts and bruises in the accident, enough for his police to get him treated immediately. He then asked them to take him to Amelia's apartment. He was anxious to know that she hadn't been hurt but wasn't quite prepared for the news he was about to hear.

When Amelia told him that they were having a baby, he said she would have to return to England before she began to show. It was imperative that his father did not get to know. It would mean dreadful trouble. They came up with a plan that Amelia would give notice to leave her position due to family problems in the UK.

Sheikh Abdulla stormed into her office. He had read her letter of resignation and would not accept it.

"Miss Amelia. I do not want you to leave. You cannot leave. I will not allow it," he demanded.

"But Your Highness," begged Amelia. "My father is very ill. I need to see him because he is very ill. I will return once I have seen him," she falsely promised.

Sheikh Abdulla turned to one of his guards and told him to go and fetch Miss Amelia a Ferrari.

"Ok, you can drive. I will bring you a car. I will give you the licence. What colour do you want?"

"But, Your Highness ….."

Tareef's absence from her office was conspicuous in the forthcoming days and weeks. Amelia knew that he was afraid of the responsibility of fatherhood, particularly with an English woman. She also knew that to him she was a commoner and a wife would already have been selected for him, not that marriage had entered her head. She was merely having fun.

Afraid of the time when her baby would show, Amelia had to think of another plan to escape the country. She realised what serious trouble she would encounter if the truth was revealed. Sheikh Abdulla was already refusing to let her go – even to see her allegedly ill father – so she had to work hard to free herself from his control.

A thick envelope had been pushed under the door of her apartment containing a set of keys. She didn't quite understand until she saw the bright red Ferrari parked outside. This was going to be really difficult.

She arrived at the office in the official limousine as usual only to be confronted by two hefty men in white regalia claiming to be secret police. They wanted her passport 'to check the visa and to stamp it!' Foolishly, but under duress, Amelia fished it out of her handbag and handed it over. This was a huge mistake.

On the orders of the Sheikh, his men had confiscated her passport. She could not leave the country. Tareef was nowhere to be seen apparently gone to Cairo to meet with a friend. Amelia had no-one in whom she could confide. She was alone and trapped.

She continued to work in her usual efficient way giving no opportunities for complaints about her. Her only means of escape would be for her friend

Mandy to call the Sheikh and, with her beautiful film-star voice, persuade him to let her go to see her father on the promise that she would return. But, how could she phone Mandy when she had no access to a telephone? She knew that the phones in the palace would be tapped.

That evening, alone in her apartment, she thought about the telephone engineer who had offered to allow her to make free calls to England. She hadn't thought to take up his offer and didn't know how to contact him. She had encountered him at Terry's offices and didn't want to go back there begging.

She had full access to the telex machine in her own office within the palace but wasn't sure whether it was monitored and anyway Mandy didn't have a machine on which to receive that type of message. She was stumped.

There was Al. They had parted on good terms. He had been a good friend and played the part of a husband during those weeks when they shared the house. She could drive the Ferrari to his brother's home in the hopes of seeing him, also hoping that the car wasn't being tracked.

After driving up and down sandy back-streets, she eventually found the road and parked the beauty outside the doors of Al's brother's home. She banged on the old double-doors hoping that someone would hear her but it, instead, alerted the neighbours who came out into the street talking amongst themselves, looking at her then looking at the car. Such opulence had never visited this area prior to this woman arriving.

Eventually Al opened the door and quickly took her inside. He put his fingers to his lips indicating that she should be quiet as his brother was at home and didn't know about her existence. She didn't realise at the time, but his brother would not have approved of him having a friendship with an English girl.

She asked him to swear to secrecy that he wouldn't divulge what she was about to tell him. He agreed and she shared the facts with him. She needed help. How could he help? Would the friend who gave him the wine be able to help? Afterall, that was an unlawful thing to do – hand wine to a Muslim.

He said he would need some time to do something and that he would keep in touch. They agreed to meet again next Friday, their day of rest, and he hoped by then he would have some kind of solution.

Feeling that she could trust him, she sped off in the Ferrari much to the astonishment of the large gathering of young men who had huddled around the car to kick its tyres and imagine themselves sporting such a vehicle. And a woman was driving!

The following Friday Amelia met Al at the appointed time and venue out of town. Her heart was pumping furiously as she waited to hear the plan.

Al told her to have her bags packed and to be ready to be picked up from her apartment at 4am the following day. This was quite a shock to Amelia, as such short notice wasn't what she had expected.

"What about my passport?" she asked him. "I can't leave the country without it."

"I know," replied Al. "It is all taken care of. I will collect you from your apartment and will give your passport to you at that time."

"How?"

"My friend, he works for the Sheikh. He loves me very much and will do what I ask from him. I tell him that the police they took your passport and he knows about it. It was his friend who took it, so he will get it from him and give it to me. It's ok. The friends, they work this way in this country."

Amelia wasn't sure whether this was all a dreadful dream. Dream or not, that evening she prepared for her assignment by packing up her belongings in readiness for the 4am start. She couldn't sleep knowing that this escapade was dangerous.

A few minutes before 4am Amelia crept across to the window and looked down upon the brightly lit street. Cars were still racing up and down so there was an element of noise at that time. She saw the headlights of a pickup stop outside the apartment block and recognised Al getting out. She looked around the room one last time, picked up her heavy suitcase, closed the door quietly pushing the keys under, by which time Al had arrived and took her luggage.

Once in the pickup they headed for the airport. Amelia was nervous and asked for the passport which Al took from his pocket and handed to her. She scrutinised it from cover to cover to check that it was indeed hers. It appeared to be a real passport and not a fake. She didn't have a ticket for the return journey! But Al had taken care of that too. He had purchased a ticket for her so with all her paperwork held tightly she only had to get through the airport check out and wait.

Reimbursing Al for the ticket didn't enter her head and he didn't ask. She jumped out of the pickup at the airport and ran inside with Al behind, carrying her case. They said a quick goodbye without kissing in public and she hurried to the checkout desk leaving him standing in the doorway. It was all so quick.

She couldn't relax until she was on that plane. What if one of the security guards, or the police recognised her? What if she was arrested? What if ......

The passengers were called to board the same Boeing 747 that had brought her to this country. The same plane she thought had a hot exhaust pipe! She was now ready to leave this great adventure but was taking home a souvenir who would last a lifetime – her precious baby.

A tenant was occupying Amelia's house on her return to the UK. She had no alternative other than to stay with an old friend whom she had met in the days when she had taken on the title of 'masseuse.'

Toby was a bachelor who had looked after his old mother acquiring their little terraced house once she had passed away. He sold it and purchased a ground floor maisonette with two bedrooms. He was more than happy to allow Amelia to stay and although her pregnancy was never discussed, as she grew bigger it was obvious. Toby was autistic and had been moderately obsessed with Amelia since meeting her at the clinic. He was more than proud to have this beautiful young lady staying with him. Perhaps in his mind, he hoped that the neighbours thought she was his girlfriend.

Amelia registered with a new doctor in Rosedale and kept an appointment towards the end of July. She had met up with Alice, her old schoolfriend the week before and together they had been strawberry picking in the fields near Alice's home. Alice had, by this time, another child just three months old.

Amelia was called to see the doctor and invited to lie on the couch to be examined. As the doctor poked around, she screamed in pain.

"You, my lady, are in labour!" explained the doctor.

"Labour? What does that mean?" questioned Amelia who had not the faintest idea of the procedure of childbirth. She had been a career girl. Domesticity or motherhood wasn't in her dictionary.

"It means, quite bluntly, that we are going to get you an ambulance to the hospital where you will give birth to a child!" the doctor retorted. She wasn't sure if his remarks were sarcastic or not. Her mind was somewhere else.

"No! I don't need an ambulance. I can drive!" she explained thinking about her Morgan car being parked on the roadside outside the surgery.

"If you do that, we take no responsibility for you whatsoever," said the doctor sternly.

She struggled off the bed and left the surgery.

The short journey from the surgery to the hospital was purgatory. The wooden chassis of the car exaggerated every bump. She squeezed her buttocks together hoping to keep the baby inside her until she could park the car.

Fear struck her like lightning. She turned the key in the lock and waddled to the hospital entrance. In her naivety she walked with her legs open thinking the baby was going to drop at any moment.

Having been observed by hospital staff, a wheelchair was brought to the door to take her to a room off the main maternity ward where she was left alone for several hours.

The walls of the old hospital were cracked and marked. The doors were chipped where endless beds and wheelchairs had scraped off the paint over the years. An old washbasin was situated in the corner of the room next to a machine with monitor and tubes connected near her bed.

She waited for what seemed hours. In fact, it probably was hours because it wasn't until the early hours of the morning that her little baby decided to enter this world. The tiny weeny little boy was premature and the midwives tried to ascertain how old he actually was.

Amelia was allowed to cuddle him before he was swiftly taken into the Special Care unit and incubated. He was to stay there for five weeks until he reached the weight of five pounds. During this time Amelia could breast feed him a few times, but the nurses also extracted milk to drip feed him.

All new to her, it was frightening having a machine clamped to her breast squeezing like a pump, hurting because of her tenderness.

The tenant in her home refused to move out. Amelia was homeless. Again? She couldn't take a new baby out of the hospital and certainly couldn't take him back to Toby's small maisonette. She was now faced with another problem.

Alice and her husband Andrew were the only visitors she received and they only visited once. Alice's sister had knitted some doll's clothes for the unnamed baby and Alice promised to pass on all her son's small clothes as he was three months older.

After staying five weeks in the hospital, receiving no visitors and hearing all the other delighted parents oooing and aaaahing over their new babies, Amelia felt very lonely and unhappy. She hadn't expected to hear from Tareef but had hopes in her heart that he might have tried to make contact. So understandably when she was told that she could be discharged with baby, she couldn't wait to run up the ward and telephone Alice. Alice and Andrew came to fetch her from the hospital; Andrew drove Amelia's car from the carpark and Alice transported the new Mum and baby.

Miraculously Amelia had been able to arrange temporary accommodation whilst in hospital. She was one who might have been kicked down, but was quick to get up, brush off the dust and start again.

They drove into the council estate and parked the vehicles outside a two storey block of flats. The flats looked uninviting. The grey pebble-dashed walls were drab and depressing but Amelia knew this was not for ever. Notice had been served on her tenant so he would be leaving in one month. She could surely bear this for a short time.

Alice and Andrew had thrown a rug into the one room and provided her with a table, chair and bed. They borrowed a cot from a friend and with the basic necessities Amelia needed to make the best of a bad situation. Alice handed Amelia a big bag of baby clothing as they kissed goodbye.

Amelia closed the door behind them. Silence roared through the tiny room. She held her son in her arms, a warm little bundle. She was afraid.

'I am now responsible for you,' she whispered to him. 'Your little life is in my hands and I promise to love and care for you.'

The telephone line had been connected and through her contact with Al, had asked him to forward her number to Tareef. She trusted Al to do this because he was such a lovely person. But, she didn't hear from the father of her son. She was, afterall, a commoner. It was easy for him to wipe his hands and walk away.

Six weeks passed and Amelia was informed by the agent that her tenant was leaving the property at the end of the week. She wanted to inspect the house before moving out of the temporary accommodation she had been given.

As soon as her house was vacant, she travelled to inspect. The familiar road seemed the same as it had before she had gone abroad. Once inside she began to envisage how she would decorate it - where her little baby would sleep – how she would change everything around and make it into a proper home for them.

Driving the baby in a carrycot on the floor of her Morgan was not appropriate. He was being juggled about and she was very much aware that she needed to change the car. She had made a lot of money by working abroad and decided to buy a used Renault which could be bashed about without worrying about the paintwork, or where it was parked. So, this she did.

She needed to give this little boy a name. Time was running out and she had to register his birth. She thought hard about naming him suitably and wanted desperately to give him his father's name. She had fallen in love with Tareef despite their affair being so brief. She was heartbroken that he had dumped her and his son. There were times when her tears fell on the small child's face as she sobbed whilst feeding him.

She walked into the Registry Office and was attended by a young man. With self-assertion she made the proclamation that her son would be called Edward Stanton. The registrar asked if she was sure that she wanted to call him this name. She was sure. He was Edward.

Once they were settled in their own little home, Amelia set about painting and decorating, skills which she had learned and not been taught. She painted a nursery rhyme scene on the white wall in the hall, just at skirting level so that when Edward could crawl he could look at it. She devoted every minute of her time to this little boy.

This was true love. Love from the depths of her heart. She knew this because she had known it only once before but recognised it as raw, unconditional love. But this was different. Instead of being her only lover, this love was the true love of her life.

Her love life had turned full circle. It started when her heart missed a beat upon seeing Rob across the room on her first day at college. Instantly she knew that this tall, dark-haired, extremely handsome fellow in a sports jacket was going to be "hers!"

Amelia's home life was unhappy. She had a loveless childhood. Her mother was young and inattentive. Her means of escape was to go away to college, miles away from home. It meant a lot of travelling but that suited Amelia because she spent less time at home.

It was her first day and Induction Day. All students were called into a huge room where they would receive information about the college and about the courses they were about to undertake.

Amelia sat alone at a desk at the back of the room. This was a good observation point as she could see all the students arriving and taking places to sit in readiness for the lecture. A tall girl with black hair in a plait down to her waist and wearing a red jacket approached Amelia asking if anyone was going to sit beside her. Amelia beckoned for her to sit with her. Little did she know that Alice would become a lifelong friend.

Amelia's eyes followed Rob as he walked with a group of others to the other end of the room. He had no idea that he was being stalked but Amelia owned him.

The winter of 1962-1963 was the coldest on record with snowfalls lasting several months. It was called The Big Freeze.

It actually began on Boxing Day 1962 so the college reopened as usual after the Christmas break. It soon became clear that the snow was going to close businesses, railways, roads etc but not even the weathermen predicted that it would last until March 1963.

Power cuts caused the college to close. Students steadily returned home after being told that it would be closed until further notice.

Alice offered for Amelia to stay with her because the transport system had broken down. Snow was falling rapidly and freezing as it touched the earth. Amelia was very grateful to receive the kind offer but having struck up several conversations with Rob over the term, preferred to take up his invitation to go to his house. His mother worked in her own shop and so would not be at home.

They walked hand in hand up the hill towards the station. Trains were now at a stand still and passengers were huddled together under shelters waiting to be picked up by other means.

Amelia was safe in Rob's strong hands. The slippery footpath proved no danger to her. If she stumbled, he held her. She knew she was in love with this "man." He was a gentleman. He knew so much more than she did. She was able to respect him.

They arrived at his bungalow and he took her through the small kitchen into the sitting room and on to the bedroom which he shared with his younger brother. The room was dark, yet he closed the blinds on both windows. Two single beds were placed at either side of the room with a table in between. He turned on a light by the bedside and began to undress Amelia taking off her blouse and tenderly touching her shoulders as he loosened her bra. Their lust and passion exploded. They couldn't wait. She was fifteen – he was seventeen. He was experienced. He had a girlfriend, but she would soon be history.

Lying on the bed in all her nakedness Amelia gave herself to him. She knew this was right. He was the person with whom she wanted to spend the rest of her life.

He took her to the bathroom and bathed her parts tenderly with sweet smelling soap. Taking a rough towel, he dried her gently as one might dry a baby. Going into the kitchen, he then poured out neat gin for her to drink – as a precaution, he said. She had never tasted alcohol and told him that the gin had 'gone off!' He laughed. She was so naïve and unworldly.

He offered to walk with Amelia the three miles to Alice's house. He knew where it was situated because his aunt lived close by. Amelia didn't know the town and was grateful that he knew directions and grasped his hand once again as they began to walk. Her feelings were mixed because she didn't want to leave him. She wanted to stay with this strong, man forever. They were now bonded. He was protective and attentive, gentle and loving. He was everything.

During the time they shared at college their relationship grew. They became entwined and of course Amelia was experiencing love for the first time in her life. Rob finished his relationship with his older girlfriend and took their relationship seriously. Whenever they had the opportunity they would show their love for each other. Passing on the stairs as they moved from one lecture to another, they would touch hands. Rob's friends knew that they were 'together.'

Occasionally Rob borrowed his mother's Triumph Herald car and they would drive out into the country to find a quiet spot to demonstrate their love at its deepest and in no time at all they graduated from college. Rob took an apprenticeship with a local company learning how to measure and fit carpets. Amelia, on the other hand, made a decision which would change her life. She left home.

On the first day away from home, she secured her first proper job with a solicitors' practice in Stourton and on the second day found some lodgings. On the third day she began working.

She settled well into her first position as Shorthand Typist in the partnership. Her boss, an ex-Army Major, was extremely quiet and, she thought, rather shy.

He sported a large moustache, stood upright and his deep voice was soft. His office was located on the first floor of the old building on the opposite side of the steep stairs leading to Amelia's small room. When he required her services, to take down shorthand dictation, he rather used the internal telephone to summon her.

At first Amelia was nervous and worried about being able to read back her outlines. The jargon used was unfamiliar to her to begin with, but she soon understood the phrases used in conveyancing and quickly became very competent at drawing up the legal documents without help.

The Senior Partner's Secretary was older than Amelia and shared the office downstairs with another Secretary and a Junior. She was planning to get married so the office was usually filled with chit-chat about the forthcoming wedding arrangements. Although Amelia appeared interested because she wanted to fit in, she soon became aware that she was an outsider.

It was apparent by the way in which the Office Junior 'forgot' to bring her coffee or when she did, reluctantly thumped the cup on the desk spilling the contents. Amelia wasn't aware of anything she had done to deserve the hostility being dished up.

This was her new life. She was now free and still, the feeling of being an outsider was capturing this freedom.

Rob was everything to Amelia. Her soul-mate. She was able to open her heart to him. There was nothing hidden. She talked about her unhappiness at work but he simply dismissed it as them being jealous of her. Jealous? How could they be jealous of her, she thought. She didn't understand.

Each morning as she walked across the park, over the dewy grass and into the town towards the office, she wondered where her life was taking her. Since leaving home she had experienced only an element of freedom but was this *true* freedom?

Although she had secured a room in an old lady's home as a paying lodger, she spent most of her time with Rob who was her reason for living. Her room was dark and although it was the first bedroom she had ever had of her own, it had 'something' about it which she didn't like. The wardrobe and dressing table were made of dark oak and felt dark too. Mrs Cotton was a widow of uncertain years who had never moved an item in the house since her husband's death. Although her son and grandsons visited often as they lived close by, they hadn't been able to influence her to move on in her bereavement. Being sensitive, Amelia was picking up on something which she didn't quite understand but knew wasn't nice. As often as she could, she would stay out late so that she only had to sleep there.

One night she was wakened by someone calling her by name. She heard it clearly and woke up with a start, but old Mrs Cotton was sound asleep and there were no other occupants in the house. Amelia was afraid. She knew, without a doubt, that *someone* had called her.

When she saw Rob the following day after work, she told him and they both decided that she should look for somewhere else to live.

Settled in her job and earning a regular salary, she was able to afford to take a one-bedroom apartment only two doors below the office in the same street. The flat was fully furnished and, naturally, Amelia was delighted. This was her first real home.

She packed up her clothing, the only belongings she possessed, thanked Mrs Cotton and ran out to Rob in the waiting car, ready to take her on another chapter of life's journey.

Her boss, Mr Dorkins, or Major Dorkins as most called him, wasn't hostile towards her. He was just a quiet man – a gentleman of the old school. He didn't complain about the standard of her work because it was without fault. He often called her to sit opposite him at his large desk and while he shuffled his papers about she waited for him to dictate, but he often didn't. She sighed a little, but, being young, and this being her first experience of work, thought little of it.

Amelia found the conveyancing work really interesting. She learned how to draw up a conveyance document of property or land without any assistance from anyone and soon Mr Dorkins was just giving her the background information, allowing her to produce the documents for signature by both parties. He trusted her.

It had been suggested that, should she continue to work at the practice for ten years, she could then qualify for an articleship and become a solicitor. This opportunity appealed to her, but ten years was a long, long time and she couldn't make such a commitment with the uncertainty of not knowing how her life was to unfold.

Things between the upstairs and downstairs offices became tense and deteriorated to such a degree that eventually the girls downstairs were not even speaking to Amelia. This distressed her and she decided to make an appointment to speak with the Senior Partner.

Mr Andrews was a small, bald headed man who invited her into his vast, dark, front office to sit on a chair placed strategically before him.

"Hello Amelia. How are you getting on? You have now been with us for over twelve months – are you enjoying your work?" he smiled. "I hear very good reports from Mr Dorkins."

This was the first occasion during the year in which she had worked for them that Mr Andrews had actually spoken to Amelia other than touching the brim of his hat and uttering 'Good morning' if they ever saw each other on the doorstep in the morning.

"I am enjoying my work very much, thank you Mr Andrews," replied

Amelia. "There is something which I should like to bring to your attention, though ….."

"Oh yes?" enquired Mr Andrews as he shuffled paperwork from his in-tray to his out-tray. Amelia didn't really think he was particularly interested in having a conversation with her.

"I don't think the staff here like me. They are making things very difficult …."

Mr Andrews looked up over his spectacles, "Whatever do you mean?" He was clearly agitated.

"As I said, Sir, things are being made very difficult for me."

"Well I think you are being too sensitive," he brushed it off and with a wave of his hand gesticulated that the meeting was over.

Although she enjoyed her work there and had been promoted from Junior Shorthand Typist to Senior Shorthand Typist, she still felt unfulfilled. Her responsibilities had increased and she was now able to produce Conveyance Engrossments, Wills, Codicils, Deeds of Gift – her work covering a broader spectrum but the situation regarding the downstairs staff had become intolerable and she was becoming very unhappy.

The Senior Partner's Secretary got married and invited everyone from the office except Amelia. It couldn't have been more obvious that she was an outsider. Memories of her unhappy childhood began to surface. She looked for another job.

Amelia thought the interview went well. Mr Booton was a short, tubby man, immaculately dressed in a well-tailored grey suit. His beautiful, short white hair showed off a tanned face. He was a very busy person, constantly moving papers or pacing up and down the room. His 'busyness' earned him the nick-name of Bunny Rabbit which of course was only spoken behind his back.

Mr Booton liked her. She was well presented and spoke well despite her poor education. Perhaps it was inherited paternal generational lineage! She had learned how to dress well and was attractive. Her dark hair framed a pretty face and green eyes flashed charismatically drawing attention like a magnet.

"I will write to you at the end of the week Miss Stanton, informing you of my decision," he said as he held his chin in his hand, gently rubbing his smoothly shaved face.

Amelia rose to leave and extended her hand towards him. He took it and shook it vigorously. Had the deal been done?

As promised, at the end of the week, Amelia received an envelope with her name typed upon it. She opened it with trepidation and so hoped that she had been accepted for the role.

Her eyes cast swiftly over the first paragraph to the words, 'I have pleasure to offer you the position of Personal Assistant to myself …..'

Her journey continued – the highway was ahead.

It was, with elation, that Amelia gave Mr Andrews her written resignation notice. He didn't appear to be surprised and showed no signs of regret. She walked quietly up the back stairs to her office. She would have to tell Major Dorkins before Mr Andrews broke the news to him.

Her heart beat loudly, knocking between her ribs and the walls of her chest. She hadn't felt quite like this since childhood. With a surge of strength she tapped on the Major's office door and waited.

"Come in!"

"Good morning Major."

"Good morning Miss Stanton."

"Major – I just want you to know that I am leaving ...."

He stood up with a jolt. Perhaps he thought he was still in the army standing to attention. His chair fell behind him. He reached awkwardly to retrieve it.

"Why Miss Stanton?"

"I have received an offer of promotion, Major, and would be silly not to take advantage of it," she explained quietly.

"Oh quite! Quite!" he looked bewildered.

"And, Major, you know it hasn't been good here for a long time. The other girls don't speak to me. I have been unhappy for a long time," Amelia went on to explain.

Like a wooden, mechanical doll he walked stiffly towards her with both arms outstretched. He touched her on both shoulders and kissed her cheek with a childish peck. He had only ever done that once before when he had shocked Amelia by his actions. This time she looked up into his face and noticed tears falling down his cheeks. She had no idea that she had had such an impact on his life, but, nevertheless, the time was obviously right for her to move on.

Amelia arrived at the office on her first morning in plenty of time to be introduced to the members of staff. The auctioneers were also estate agents and managers of large country estates. Apart from administrative staff there were two telephonists who operated a plug board from the reception area. They looked after reception as well as answering and getting calls for staff. Two surveyors had offices on the first floor; estate managers and articled young men from wealthy families were also employed in various other capacities. It appeared to be a family of well-connected, well-heeled friends.

The two senior partners had new offices purpose-built in an extension at the rear of the large four storey building. Adjacent to each of the new offices was a connecting room to their P.A.'s – one of which was allocated to Amelia.

She was shown to her office and the other partner's secretary appeared, introduced herself then began to familiarise Amelia with some of the procedures. A beautiful electric typewriter sat on the new desk. Amelia gasped! The old Olivetti manual machine that she had bashed for the last couple of years was now a thing of the past!

She was familiar with the IBM Golf Ball typewriter which had a pivoting type element (frequently called a 'typeball') that could be changed to display different fonts in the same document. It also replaced the traditional typewriter's moving carriage with a paper roller (platen) that stayed stationary while the typeball and ribbon mechanism moved from side to side. She had occasionally used such a machine at college as a reward for good marks at the end of the week.

As she settled into her new routine, Amelia became more organised and was asked to accompany Mr Booton on appointments to country estates and gentlemen's houses where they would take inventories of valuable antique furniture and clocks or take details of items to be included in auctions.

She soon began to recognise and learn about antique pieces as she handled ormolu clocks and precious jardinières. Beautiful gold jewellery was described in language only the experts could use. She enjoyed this so much and was able to talk about her adventures when she met with Rob in the evenings. Together they had lots to discuss.

Occasionally Amelia was required to attend the auctions and help with the administration. She often had tense moments just before her boss slammed down the gavel on a sale. There was always so much going on that she was fully occupied and able to learn more.

Apart from the auction side of the business, Amelia got involved in the estate agency part as Mr Booton was also a qualified surveyor and valuer. She accompanied him on visits to houses which were to be put on the market and watched how he took measurements, then prepared an appraisal. It wasn't long before she was being sent out alone to collate this information herself which she then formatted to produce sale brochures. Mr Booton always had the final decision on value, but he asked Amelia first for her opinion to evaluate her estimations. She was never far wrong much to his impression.

Rob owned a grey A35 van which he used for his work. He became a qualified carpet fitter, working for a large company in the home of carpet manufacturing. It was in this van that Amelia learned to drive properly.

Her only encounters with driving had been as a child, changing gear for Grandpa while he manoeuvred the pedals. Amelia applied early for a provisional driving license which would enable her to learn to drive on the roads on her seventeenth birthday.

Rob was a patient teacher and explained in great detail the workings of the car. Once she understood this, logic fell into place and at every opportunity she took to the wheel of the little grey Austin.

Amelia booked a double lesson with a professional driving instructor on the day of her driving test. The instructor was a middle-aged stout fellow with a Birmingham accent. Amelia found it hard to understand all he said as he was almost always breathless and a chain smoker so his words were punctuated with gasps and puffs on his cheap Park Drive cigarette. However, she familiarised herself with the controls of the shiny new red Hillman Imp, adjusted the driver's seat and listened carefully to her instructions. The engine of the car was located in the rear but wasn't apparent and wasn't a significant issue for the test.

"To engage the gear, you gotta push yer foot right down on the clutch. The clutch is the one on the left. Got it?"

She had got it! She moved the vehicle forward and drove slowly along the busy road trying to remember to look in the mirror, change gear, steer to the right …. This shiny new car felt so different from the well-worn, much travelled little Austin whose windscreen was higher and smaller than the instructor's Hillman.

She had booked the two hours' session to include using the vehicle for her driving test. The first hour was really only to get used to the vehicle; the intention only to use it for the test. It was more roadworthy than Rob's van and, in any case, Rob would be using his so it wouldn't be available for her.

It was pure delight as Amelia took the "L" plates off the van!

Rob and Amelia often drove out into the hills to spend time with David and June, their married friends who were much older. David and June were in their twenties and lived in a lovely bungalow set on a hill overlooking miles of countryside. Although they had been married for a long time they hadn't thought of starting a family. Their two Alsatian dogs were their substitute children.

David was a motor mechanic and had mentioned that a little A30 was for sale for thirty five pounds. Rob thought it would be an ideal car for Amelia so they purchased it after David had looked over it and approved it as being roadworthy.

Amelia took possession of the A30 on the day on which she passed her driving test. She called the car, "ROF" after its registration number, ROF 563.

For the first time, ever, she sat in the driver's seat alone and began her first journey of total freedom. Her foot pressed further and further on the accelerator pedal. She glanced at the speedometer – the needle was moving upward slowly – 80mph! The little black car had been fitted with an A35 engine (bigger than the original) so she had more power at her fingertips.

As the exhaust ripped through the silencer she was exhilarated. She was free! This was simply indescribable – freedom as the world saw it. Heavenly to Amelia at that time in her life.

She threw the little car round bends, accelerating out of them as Rob had shown her. She was at one with the little beast, sensitive to its sound and feel, as she had vowed to be since her experiences with a friend who laboured her Standard 8 insensitive to its cries leading to death in a scrap yard. None of that for Amelia! She was making herself 'one' with the machine. The engine was sheer simplicity. She changed the plugs and checked it over regularly as it was so easy to work on. She loved it dearly as one might love a pet.

Approaching the bridge that connected the two counties with her old village, signalling, she turned left and entered the main street. Looking to see if anyone noticed her, she sped up the street and turned the bend by the Crow Pub where she had 'fallen in love' with Nobby Clarke all those years ago when she was about twelve! Past the Square – she didn't need a bus now – and right into Grove Road.

It seemed strange to be driving her own car up this road; the road which she had walked up and down so many times carrying her mother's shopping, wrestling with a drunken father and running away from the threat of the broom handle across her legs.

Changing down to second gear, she swung through the gate, past the water pump and into the yard bringing the hot little car to a halt beside the air raid shelter. Slamming closed the door, Amelia walked down the pathway which served as a right of way for the neighbour, and knocked upon the old kitchen door.

Her mother half-opened the door and peered around it.

"Oh, what brings you here?" she retorted not showing any signs of gladness to see her daughter.

"I came to see you because I passed my driving test this morning and can drive!" Amelia blurted out with excitement.

"Well, are you coming in?" asked her mother making no reaction.

"Ok, but not for long. I only wanted you to know that I can drive now!"

"Mrs Rhodes died," said mother.

Amelia felt she had succeeded at something, despite her mother's negative reaction and nothing was going to steal this joy in her heart. Nothing.

Once released from the hold of the family and the village, she grasped her new life with both hands and sped away, waving to the chestnut trees, the hospital and all that living in that village had meant.

Eventually Rob became unsettled in his job as a carpet fitter and decided to start his own business. He had an established list of valuable contacts, knew how to purchase carpets from the manufacturers at good prices and had ready-made premises at the bottom of their garden. He installed industrial sewing machines in the sheds which for many years had served as a sweet factory operated by his grandfather.

The sewing machines were driven by hand along a set of ropes the length of the room. Carpets which needed to be sewn were hung from the ropes with strong clamps enabling one to run the sewing machine horizontally along the seams. It was heavy work and quite difficult if a pattern was involved because care had to be taken to match it all up.

Rob and Amelia talked about how they could take the business forward. At such early stages, they couldn't afford to employ anyone, but it wasn't the type of business only one person could manage. If Rob was out fitting, someone had to take the phone calls and do the sewing. After a lot of discussion Amelia handed in her notice to her employer. She was going to help Rob. She could do the administration side of the business as well as some of the sewing.

Mr Booton, her boss, was very sorry when she handed to him her written notice. He tried to persuade her to stay, offering her a higher salary. Of course, this was very attractive to Amelia and, indeed, so were the job/career prospects, but she loved Rob and saw it as a step towards securing their future by working at a business together.

She emptied the drawers of the desk of her personal belongings leaving instructions to her successor indicating Mr Booton's likes and dislikes. The office was prepared for someone who would enjoy the work that Amelia so loved but was sacrificing.

She shook hands with Mr Booton. (There were no kisses here. Mr Booton was a highly respectable man and also Chairman of a local political party.)

After saying goodbye to the other staff, she left the building for ever.

Her journey was taking another course.

Amelia still had possession of her car, ROF, and Rob also had his grey van but as they were launching their new business they felt that a good image was necessary. They also needed a reliable vehicle which wouldn't break down.

After talking with David, who was the car expert, it was agreed that they would trade both the car and van against a new van which they could have painted with the name of the company and phone number. The deal was done and the new white, tinny-sounding Ford van was purchased. The gears were stiff and despite being new, it didn't have that newness smell of leather which Grandpa's new cars always had.

Amelia would not collect a salary whilst the company was in its embryonic stage so she decided to cut her expenses by relinquishing her flat and moving into lodgings in the next street from Rob's house where the business premises were located in his back garden.

With fewer expenses, Amelia was able to work down the garden for no remuneration. It was cold and lonely there when Rob was out fitting carpets during the day. It was only in the evenings when they worked together sewing the pieces of carpet together and matching patterns that they saw anything of each other.

Amelia was sensitive. She thought she recognised signs that she was no longer welcome on the premises. When she told Rob, he dismissed them just as he had done when she had talked about her situation at the solicitor's office.

His Grandma, who lived next door and shared ownership of the drive, cooked for the family while Rob's widowed mother now worked fulltime in the National Savings Office in town after one of the big confectionery giants bought her shop. Amelia had always been included in the family's meal times, but, suddenly, and without warning, she was excluded. Everyone else was called to eat and Amelia was told if she wanted to eat with them she would have to pay for her food. How could she? She wasn't earning anything!

There were times when there wasn't enough work to do and Amelia found she was just wasting time sitting in the cold shed waiting for phone calls that didn't come. She and Rob concluded that she should get some temporary work until business picked up and could justify her presence there.

She enrolled with a staff agency. The woman who ran the agency simply interviewed Amelia over the phone and engaged her immediately without seeing her. This was apparently her procedure for engagement which had been repeated many times. Amelia had no idea how much influence this woman would ultimately have over her life.

Her first assignment was at the Town Hall in a small river town about ten miles away. She was to work as a P.A. to the town clerk but this was a misdescription.

In order to get to and from this assignment Rob took Amelia in the morning and collected her when he was able to get to the office after his own jobs were completed.

The Town Hall was accessed by climbing a fleet of steps from the main street. Once inside the building one entered a dark, Dickensian lobby. The first door led to the town clerk's office which was a large room with high ceilings and walls lined with bookshelves heaving with dank smelling old books. A large wooden desk was positioned in the centre of the room facing the door. Behind the desk, the tall, grey-haired, chain smoking town clerk reclined in a cloud of smoke, with his feet resting upon the desk. This was his posture for most of the working hours.

Amelia was required to run across the busy street to the newsagents to purchase his cigarettes. This she did twice a day, taking the money from the petty cash tin which was kept in the general office. Her duties as a P.A. were actually those of an office junior but she didn't complain, knowing that the position was only temporary.

A large telex machine was placed immediately in front of the office door. As well as operating a small table-top telephone switchboard, her duties included those of a punching clerk (preparing tape for insertion into the high-speed telex transmitters.) This was labour intensive particularly so when she was constantly interrupted by the telephone switchboard, members of the public coming into the office, or the typing load which was put upon her at different times of the day. Usually she was given an urgent letter to type and get in the mail at short notice before the last mail collection.

Being well organised Amelia worked well under pressure but was always pleased when the end of the working day arrived. As she had no transport now, Rob continued to drive her to the office in the new van, collecting her in the evenings.

One day, unannounced, a petite woman arrived in the office introducing herself as 'Tasleem' the new 'temp'. Taken aback, Amelia enquired of the town clerk where she should send the woman who looked like a Thai child-bride, her long black hair trailing down her back, perfectly straight. Her wrinkled face showed Amelia that she was a grown woman and much older than she.

Amelia was informed that Tasleem had been engaged to help in the general office but very soon Tasleem approached Amelia for assistance.

"I haven't used this type of switchboard before – how do you use it?"

Amelia willingly gave instruction on how to operate the machine, careful to ensure that she fully understood. Tasleem was extremely quick at learning everything shown to her.

Then, she asked to be shown how to use the telex. Amelia did wonder whether she had ever worked in an office before because she was lacking in knowledge of office procedure and looked rather more suited to work in a brothel.

Rob continued to collect Amelia after work and it became apparent that he had lots of work, so much so that his day job began to run into his evenings. Amelia was accepting for she had no reason to think otherwise. Since she had taken temporary work and was spending less time at Rob's home, things were much better.

Tasleem was very inquisitive and liked to know as much about everything as she could, including Amelia's relationship with Rob.

"I see him pick you up in his van. Is it his work van?"

"Yes."

"Does he work for somebody?"

"No. We have the business together!"

A few weeks later when Rob came to pick up Amelia at the usual time, she got into the van only to be told that Rob couldn't be with her that evening.

"Have you got another job?" she naively asked believing that he was getting so busy.

"No!" was his blunt answer. "I'm seeing somebody else and won't be seeing you again!"

Was this real? Was it a dream?

Amelia felt her head swaying – her stomach churning. She grabbed the door handle to steady herself. **The End?** Surely not! It couldn't be! How?

Tasleem had made a note of the phone number from the side of Rob's van and called him without Amelia's knowledge. She had not only stolen professional information from Amelia, but also her boyfriend – the love of her life. Amelia now had no reason to live. Her world was over – there was no future. Everything had collapsed around her. She was alone. Alone without a car, without a job, without a home. For what? For "love?"

It was to be a very long time before Amelia's heart would heal – not months, not years, but almost a lifetime. Rejection entered through the gates of her heart and made its home there.

For over three months she couldn't work. Her broken heart tormented, she cried and pined. She gave up her room in the lodging house near to Rob's home. She wasn't able to afford it anyhow. She went back to Grandpa and Grandma who now lived very close to her parents.

It was Christmas Day 1967. There wasn't any purpose for her to get up at all. Her life was empty. It was strangely comforting to overlook a busy street. The constant hum of traffic and voices reminded Amelia that there was a world out there even if hers had collapsed around her.

She thought of families all getting together today and being 'happy' however happiness is defined. She imagined children waking up early and opening presents, the smell of birds being cooked and glistening lights, all millions of miles away from her circumstances.

She looked around the sitting room. Basically furnished with old but comfortable furniture, she sat on the thick beige woollen carpet. The people next door were moving around and she could hear whistling to the sound of music.

As she buried her head in her hands, her long dark hair fell over her face and caught the drips of her salty tears. *'Why? Why? Why?'*

She looked around to see what she could find to kill this pain. There was a bottle of Johnnie Walker whisky which had been sitting in the kitchen for months. She took it and with both hands twisted the cap and poured out a generous amount into the only glass she owned.

The warm, silky smooth liquid slithered down her throat rewarding her with a heady relaxed mind. It was good. She poured another and another. The room began to sway a little but she didn't mind that and walked over to the sash window to look out on to the street.

It was a cold morning, but not a 'white christmas'. A father was walking behind his two children who were learning to ride new bikes. An old man was taking his dog for a walk and two lone boys pressed their noses against the toy shop window opposite, no doubt, hoping for more!

Amelia turned away and poured more whisky into the now empty glass. This was her way of dealing with Christmas. A time when so many people were expected to be joyful, when, in reality, it was a time when more divorces were birthed, more suicides took place and more people got depression. It's a pagan festival, traditionalised and recognised world over as Christian, celebrated by unbelievers and totally commercialised. But that wasn't a serious enough reason for Amelia to be unhappy. Where was Rob? What was he doing now? Who was with him? Who had replaced her?

She poured the last few drops of the bottle into the glass, put the bottle to her lips to catch the last drops and reached for the aspirins.

Amelia's cup of tea was cold. She put the cup into the microwave, heated it up then sat again watching the flames lick the door of the burner. The red embers of the oak logs glowed while the orange flames flickered patterns across the floor. Golden sparks floated up the chimney displaying an array which reminded Amelia of the tremendous fireworks displays she had witnessed in Malta all those years ago.

She was relaxing on the flat roof when the earth shook and a thunderous rumbling filled the air. She jumped up and saw the sky on the horizon filled with black smoke. A fireworks factory in the next village had exploded. Run by volunteers, these so-called factories were extremely dangerous and lacked any health and safety standards. Frequently one heard of someone's cousin or brother dying in such an explosion.

Fireworks are made to celebrate all the many saints days in that holy Christian land of Malta. She recalled the many festivals Geyta had taken her to. How was Geyta? It would be nice to know that she was alive and well no doubt with a large extended family.

When she felt better, Amelia promised herself that she would revisit Malta. Afterall, it was one of the first adventures that her lifetime had presented. But first, she must sort out her dietary needs and fathom out how to follow the diet. She needed to regain that inner strength which had evaporated.

There was something so attractive to Amelia about sitting in airport lounges. The anonymity – not having to speak to anyone with nobody knowing who she was. It was a long wait. Her beloved son, Edward, now a strikingly handsome man had taken her to the airport but the flight to Malta had been delayed twice.

The vast room sported miles of grey tiling, yards of pink/mauve and red fluorescent tube lights, multitudes of seats and yet, not too many people. Bars had been locked on the shop fronts and staff closed everything at 10pm. Time dawdled. Some coveted the massage chairs and cuddled up on them to sleep. She sat and read.

When the plane arrived in Malta she stepped out of the airport into the humid darkness of the island. Geyta, tired, but happy, clung on to her arm as they walked from Departures towards her now grown son, Fabian, the youngest of her four children. He leaned against his twenty years old Ford Sierra, proud as if it was new from the showroom. Taking Amelia's small suitcase and putting it in the boot, he secured the loose door with a piece of elastic and then started up the engine. Condensation covered the inside windows like a curtain necessitating Fabian to constantly wipe the windscreen with his hand. The wipers didn't work so they travelled with the window open so that he could reach out now and then to clear the glass.

When they arrived in the street that was home to Amelia in the days of Michael, Fabian parked outside Geyta's little front door, leaving the car running. They quickly removed the suitcase leaving the elastic flapping, said their 'chao's' and began to mount the high steps into her home. As they did so, a small woman dressed in black passed them in the lonesome street. She was off to the first mass of the day.

Although the structure of her little home hadn't changed, there had been alterations afterall it had been many years since Amelia had taken shelter here. Geyta now had a telephone! So, after ringing round all her friends to inform them that her best friend Amelia was going to stay in her home, she suggested taking the bus to Valletta.

By this time Amelia was wide awake and happy to go to Valletta the capital city of Malta. They walked along Carmel Street into the square passing pleasantries with the lady sitting on a milk crate outside her little shop. Past the huge church of St Catherine they hurried down the main street to the bus park where two buses were waiting.

Geyta showed her bus pass to the driver and paid the few cents for Amelia's fare. They then sat together to make the bumpy journey. The cab of the bus was covered with 'holy pictures' and a huge rosary swung from the middle of the split windscreen beneath a big wooden cross.

The driver made the sign of the cross on his body and then began the drive to Valletta. They went through several villages on the way – Kirkop where Geyta's aunty's nephew lived with a woman twice his age; under the airport runway to Luqa where Lucu had a job once; Marsa where her friend's husband looked after the race horses; the famous furniture town of Hamrun which Amelia would never, ever forget, Pieta and Floriana. After about thirty minutes they arrived at the City Gate Bus Terminus and entered through the city gate at the top of Triq ir Repubblika joining the throngs of people also entering the town.

Amelia was aware of the many changes that had taken place since she was last there. Seating areas had been built and some buildings had been demolished making way for new projects. The road had been paved with stone; lottery shops littered the street. Taking a glimpse inside, every lottery shop was similar. A long corridor really, with a glass booth erected just inside the large barn-style wooden doors. Myriads of bills were posted on the inside of the doors which, when opened, were exposed to the street. Advertisements for bingo, lotto, the superbowl prize, the snowball prize, rollover prizes – this was, indeed, a gambling nation.

The sun was hot and Amelia began to feel tired. They found a small café opposite the Law Courts which was dark and cool inside, so they sat there to drink Kinnie. Amelia had never forgotten how bitter sweet it was. After catching up and fully refreshed they decided to walk towards the bus station to catch the 34 bus to take them back to Zurrieq. Amelia was aware that their visit was short, but the heat was intense having just arrived from rain-soaked England.

They were able to board the bus as the engine was already running. It was a different bus taking them back but was decorated similarly with rosaries, white plastic roses, a huge crucifix and a picture of Madonna attached to the roof of the cab. The ritual of blessing himself was taken seriously by the driver before he shoved the vehicle into gear and they shuddered off.

On the return journey, Amelia could see from the window the extraordinary names of some of the houses : Holy Family, Shalom (with two big buddhas in the garden) 25th November, St Katherine, Holy Mother etc. The bigger the statue in the small garden indicated the closer to God they thought they were!

As they drove through Msida the huge church dominated the skyline. Scaffolding had been erected around it and work was progressing. It appeared to be a new build to Amelia. When she questioned Geyta, she explained that for a long time they couldn't complete the building because they ran out of money, but the ''church'' won the lottery so they are now able to complete the building work!

Travelling past another church in Paola they saw an old woman busy sweeping the steps outside the building. This was an outward show of her dedication to the church, earning her wages to heaven. Amelia was told that the inside of the woman's own home was neglected and dirty, but in the eyes of passers-by, she was a good woman seen to be doing 'good works!'

Amelia was seated by the window and noticed that traffic was particularly heavy on the opposite side of the road. It had piled up because a poor dog had been hit by a car and left injured in the road. Maltese people are mostly afraid of dogs so consequently nobody felt brave enough to help the animal. Cars began to drive around him as he yelped and writhed in the road. Amelia was quite upset by this and then the screeching of brakes resulted in somebody crashing into the back of one of the queued cars. Drivers didn't seem to pay much attention to their driving, lacking concentration especially if they get distracted. Animals were so disregarded in Malta often tied up on flat roofs in the scorching sunshine with no shade. Their lives seem to have no purpose other than to bark furiously if anyone comes into their vision. It was only when Malta joined the European Union that the shooting of wild birds became unlawful. Pedestals could still be seen erected along the roadside a reminder of how they were used as bait to entice the birds to sit. Indeed, Lucu, Geyta's husband, still had caged finches. The miniscule cages hardly gave the birds space to open their wings. As it became unlawful, Lucu kept them in a dark shed out of sight so they never got to see daylight.

Once back at her home, Geyta talked on the phone whilst Amelia managed to drink a cup of tea. With gestures and a raised voice she revealed afterwards that her sister couldn't visit the hospital where her father had been taken, so she had to go. Amelia offered to go with her. It was a long day, but Amelia didn't feel too tired. They ate fig pastries with their tea then prepared to walk back to the bus park to get a bus to Siggiewi to the old hospital now served as an old folks' home.

In the meantime, Lucu released swarms of flies when he opened the shed door to feed his ten white rabbits. Caged in six crates they were fed until big enough to be killed to eat. As another means of income, he sold them in the pub perhaps keeping one back for Geyta to make the famous Maltese rabbit stew.

As they were walking up the street, Geyta and Amelia saw a middle-aged woman with greying hair step out of her home, accompanied by another woman of similar age. They were both carrying bags and acknowledged Geyta. Some conversation took place which Amelia didn't understand but Geyta explained that they, too, were going to the same hospital to visit an old relative.

A journey of about forty minutes took them to the entrance gates of a huge building, formerly the hospital, but now looking very tired, almost derelict. They walked through the grounds and into the hospital. The corridors were long and dirty. Their voices echoed as they walked for what seemed ages. No security was apparent and they were able to open locked doors easily.

At the end of a very long passageway they entered a reception area where there were about five adults sitting chatting at a desk. They didn't look up as the couple approached and entered the ward opposite them. The small room contained two beds. Geyta's father was sitting propped up in a chair next to the bed beside the door. Suffering with poor eyesight, his face lit up when Geyta spoke to him. She asked him who he thought was with her and immediately he recognised Amelia after all those years, bringing forth a wonderful smile on his pitifully thin, sad face.

The sun shone against the window where a woman sat bent over a man in the bed. They thought it would be a good idea to take Baba out into the gardens. He loved gardening and once owned a plot of land where he grew apricots, all manner of vegetables and fruits. Obviously, he missed all that and just a peek at the flowers, surely, would cheer him up.

Geyta went to find a wheelchair and brought back an old-fashioned version which they placed next to his chair. No professional help was forthcoming although they were being watched by the staff. They struggled with the small body and got him into the chair with a struggle.

Out in the garden they pointed out fruits which were growing up the walls of the old hospital and showed him the flowers growing in the beds alongside. He seemed content and managed to mumble some words to Geyta.

It became apparent that his thin body might be feeling the cold so we took him indoors after only a short walk. Once inside the ward he asked Geyta to put him to bed. Together they managed to get him from the wheelchair into the bed and covered him with a sheet. His feet were dreadfully cold. He snuggled up and they both felt it was time to leave him to sleep.

When they arrived at the hospital entrance Geyta beckoned for them to sit on the wall. She told Amelia that the husband of one of the women who travelled with them from the village, would take them back in his car. So they sat on the wall in the sunshine reflecting on Baba's condition until the ladies arrived, still carrying their bags.

They all walked along the roadway within the hospital perimeter until they reached a grey Peugeot parked awkwardly on the roadside. A large grey-haired man sat in the driver's seat while the three women got into the back. His wife then sat beside him in the front of the car with the rosary, crucifix, statue of Jesus (mounted on the dashboard) and all the stickers.

With a rev of the engine, he let out the clutch sharply, making their heads fall back into the headrests. Amelia suspected that he was angry. She was right. Geyta told her that he had moaned that he was always the one to bring them home and that the other woman's husband didn't ever offer: hence he took out his anger on the car.

He displayed an erratic driving performance, accelerating up to traffic islands and braking at the last minute. It was, perhaps, a good thing that Amelia didn't understand what he was shouting at other drivers but his fury was apparent! As they swung from side to side the statue stood proud and didn't move.

They drove into Zurrieq, swerved around the back of the village turning into narrow streets coming to a halt at the rear of a block of flats in an area of about a dozen garages. His wife, Connie, jumped out of the car and unlocked the garage door in readiness for him to park the vehicle. Geyta, the other woman and Amelia quickly got out of the car before he drove it into the garage and Amelia waited for him to get out of the vehicle. She shook hands with him and thanked him for his kindness in taking them home. She didn't want him to feel that he had been used, despite his anger.

They continued down a steep alleyway which took them to the street below Carmel Street. Geyta popped her head into a small shop tucked away insignificantly and could have been mistaken for a house. She wanted a vegetable of some kind to make a stew. Picking it from one of the crates stacked inside the shop, Geyta told the young girl that she would pay tomorrow.

Once inside her dark home, Geyta began to prepare the food for their meal. The kitchen was furnished with cast-offs from various people. The fridge-freezer was about forty years old donated by the lady in Ta'Xbiex for whom she had cleaned. Ornaments crowded the shelves of various cupboards she had inherited from people who were throwing them away. A mixture of buddhas, veiled faces of arab ladies and holy pictures adorned the crumbling walls. Sitting beside the make-shift sink was a statue of some goddess holding an incense burner between her folded legs.

Amelia was beginning to realise that she hadn't slept. Geyta told her to go and lie on the bed she had set for her in a small room off the kitchen. She had asked her son to paint it fifteen days before Amelia's arrival so the yellow paint was still fresh on the breeze blocks and hadn't yet begun to peel. A small single bed was placed alongside the wall under a deep set window. It was impossible to see through the glass because wet plaster had been slopped down it and allowed to dry. Dust had congealed on that, rendering it useless as a window!

Pretty curtains were hung at the window. They matched a piece of cloth that had been put on the bed to serve as a bedspread. New orange-coloured matching chests of drawers and wardrobe completed the furnishing of the room. A dirty blue mat covered an array of different floor tiles. Lucu had laid them, run out of a particular pattern and finished with all-sorts obtained by begging from various friends. A row of paisley type shiny tiles lay beside some plain terracotta and tiles with stars had been laid by the door. A large chandelier dominated the room but only one of the sockets held a long-life bulb and a flying santa hung by a piece of string from one of the brackets.

A mixture of soft toys, teddies and a blackboard were piled into a corner out of the way watched by a statue of St Francis of Assisi holding a lamb. There is a tale of a tamed lamb known to follow St Francis whenever he came near the lamb's home in Portiuncula.

As her eyes looked at the walls, Amelia was horrified to see a framed picture of her deceased dog, Charlie gazing down at her. She had sent a large photograph of him to Fabian some years' ago because of his fondness for dogs and they had obviously had it framed. Beside it was a similar picture of the poor dog he had held captive in the shed. Tied up for years, walking in its own mess it was as fierce as a lion. Obviously passed away too, Amelia had two dead dogs for company.

She slipped off her shoes and lay on top of the piece of cloth on the bed which was hard as nails and felt as though she was lying on a board. She nodded off for a short time and when she woke it was time to eat.

The kitchen was so hot. She had noticed a table and chairs outside the kitchen door. They had no garden, as such, but only enough space for the table between the door and shed where Geyta kept her washing machine. Amelia suggested that they ate outside. Geyta, always willing, agreed and proceeded to take the oilcloth covering off the table to reveal an off-white cotton tablecloth. She brought out a knife and fork, both had yellow handles emblazoned with "Weetabix." She had been collecting vouchers from the cereal packets being able to redeem them for knives, forks, spoons, mugs – all with the same logo! Unfortunately the cutlery was made out of soft tin and the smallest amount of pressure caused them to bend!

She placed a plate with cooked meat and chips before Amelia then went back into the kitchen to get a smaller portion for herself. The meat had been tenderised in the saucepan for hours and really was delicious although the water in which it had been cooked and purposed as a gravy was tasteless. It was fortunate that Amelia wore spectacles for without them she couldn't see much at close range.

In amongst the chips was a black foreign object. On closer examination she noticed it was a fried cockroach! Geyta had used a saucepan of oil which had been left on the side for goodness knows how long and one of the beasts had dropped into it and drowned. As the kitchen was so dark, she ignorantly just popped the chips in to fry on top of it. It took all that Amelia could muster to eat the chips. She prayed that the food would be a blessing to her body and that is all she could do. She left him on the side of her plate. Another dish of chips had been produced for them to help themselves. Geyta was insistent that she had more, but she flatly refused. At that Geyta threw the dirty blue towel which she used as a tea-towel, hand-towel, handkerchief and floor cloth, over the bowl to keep the flies off! Amelia noticed that the chips were still on the side of the primus stove the following morning (but uncovered) and were offered to her for breakfast!

The barking dogs on the roof next door woke Amelia when it was just getting light at 6:15am. Geyta was already in the kitchen boiling water to fill the thermos flask. This was done to save her from boiling the kettle. Her efforts at saving the calor gas.

Amelia put on her dressing gown and stepped out of the bedroom into the kitchen just as Geyta was about to pour a saucepan of potato water down the lavatory. Flushing the lavatory was also a great consumer of expensive water so was only done after big jobs – if they remembered! To pass urine didn't warrant a flush!

As they drank their first cups of tea and coffee, they talked about what they would do that day. Geyta wanted to go to the village Square to get fish from the fish lady who parked her van there so after a cat-lick of a wash, Amelia dressed and they walked up Carmel Street towards The Square.

The fish lady's blue van was parked outside the church. Plastic crates of fish lay in the back; a prime target for flies. She was attending to a grey-haired man and a lot of talk was taking place between them which, obviously, Amelia didn't understand. With the occasional wave of her hand to distract the flies, she picked up three huge lampouki and put them into a polybag to hand to her customer. There was more talk then she added a couple of smaller fish and waved him away.

From his body language and the bowing of his head, it appeared that he was very grateful. Amelia didn't see any exchange of money.

Turning round and wiping her bloody hands on a filthy old rag, the fish lady spoke to Geyta. From the plastic crate she picked up a lampuka and with her foot drew a bucket from underneath the van. Inside the bucket was a bloody mess of intestines. With the slight of hand she delved her nails behind the gills of the fish, pulled its inside out and threw it into the bucket which was alive with flies. She then smoothed her hand down the back of the fish and plonked it into a used polybag before giving it to Geyta for the exchange of euros. The money tin lay beside a rusty old knife which she used for stirring the cents, then picked up the cash with her bloody hands, passing it to Geyta as change.

As they walked away Amelia asked why the previous customer hadn't paid. Geyta explained that he was the priest!

Their next stop was the butcher. They walked past St Katherine's Working Men's Club and climbed the steps into the Bosom Butcher's shop opposite. The counter faced them as they entered the small shop and were welcomed by a huge poster picture of a bearded "Jesus" who dominated the wall. Shafts of gold light emanated from his body in all directions and a huge gold halo crowned his head.

The counter separated the customer from the butcher who was working on several piles of meat at the same time which he left on the side to attend to Geyta. She asked for minced beef so he selected from one of the piles and shoved it into the mincing machine. The remnants of the previous customer's meat fell on to the dish before Geyta's choice was processed leaving her first-fruits for the next customer no doubt as he didn't endeavour to clean the machine. With a rusty knife he scraped the mince from the dish into his hand to form a ball. He then reached over the piles of uncovered meat to get a plastic bag. He tried to push the ball of meat into the bag, but it was too small. Instead of disposing of it, he simply popped it on the side to use again and selected a larger bag into which the ball of meat was rolled.

Geyta popped it into her trolley bag on top of the fish and then they continued to the bakers. The baker was situated a little further up the same street. It could easily be overlooked as being a garage because the outlook to the street was simply a big wooden door.

Inside the dark room was a large wooden framed trolley on to which the bread had been placed in readiness for the oven. The oven was in the wall and extremely deep. It delved so far that one couldn't see the back of it. The baker was picking up the dough on a common or garden spade and shovelling it into the deep oven.

A small table was placed near the door where an old lady served the public by giving them the bread and taking the money which she placed in an old cardboard box on a shelf nearby. The bread was not wrapped and no doubt touched by many others before being consumed. But, it was delicious.

Back at the house Geyta took *her* rusty knife from the drawer under the sink and cut into the small round loaf. She took a tomato from the fruit dish on the table and began to smother the piece of bread with juice as she squeezed the tomato with her hands. She then reached for the olive oil but Amelia stopped her. She didn't want her bread soaked with oil so ate it with only the tomato scraped over it. Oh! It was so good!

They arranged to go to Paolo that evening to a line dancing dinner. Surprisingly Geyta organised these functions and by doing so obtained a free ticket for herself. She requested that the mini-bus be at the children's garden at the bottom of Carmel Street at 7pm. They changed their clothes and left Lucu lying on the bed watching television for that is where the TV lived – in their bedroom.

Not knowing what she was going to find, Amelia allowed Geyta to take her to the mini-bus. They were the first couple to be picked up, so she sat directly behind the driver where she was able to feel the breeze through his open window.

They drove round the network of narrow streets in Zurrieq picking up old ladies whom one would think weren't up to dancing! There was big Rita – a blonde fifty something year old. Dressed in tight, white trousers and a revealing top, she sat beside the driver. Connie and her aunt were both quiet and remained so for the whole evening. Altogether there were twelve ladies who filled the fourteen-seater mini bus. It seemed to be a long way to Paolo, but it was dark and the bus was slow.

They arrived in a side street outside a hotel where people were gathering at the foyer. Amelia followed Geyta as she seemed to know the format. As they waited inside the hotel, she distributed small pieces of paper which had 'fish' or 'chicken' written on them. Whatever their choice of meal, an appropriate slip of paper was handed over. This was to be reserved for relinquishing when the food was served which would be at about 9pm.

Long tables had been set up in the ballroom horizontal to the stage. A short well-rounded man stood on the stage with a microphone. His duties were to sing and joke throughout the evening sharing the stage with a DJ having a repertoire of seventies and eighties music, to which the happy audience would step their line-dancing skills. Amelia didn't realise that they all took it so seriously, having a different dancing format for each piece of music. She wondered how the elderly remembered it at all!

One couple, in particular, were drawn to Amelia's attention by Geyta.

"See, that man he is from where you live," she pointed to a small, slight man dressed in black complete with black cowboy hat and high-heeled boots. He was accompanied by his wife, a strawberry blonde lady, taller than he, who wore a very nicely pressed blouse with trousers.

They walked over to Geyta and Amelia to introduce themselves saying that they lived in Worminster but would love to live in Malta. In fact, they were returning to England on the same flight as Amelia but would only stay at home for two weeks before returning to Malta once more. As they danced he became entranced and floated through the steps as though high as a kite! They were both in their seventies! With promises to see Amelia again and to definitely catch up at the airport on their return, they vanished on to the dance floor to return to their dancing routine. As they crammed into the mini bus to return to Zurrieq, there was much joviality and laughter about the evening which they had all, obviously enjoyed tremendously.

It rained during the night and Amelia heard it beating on the flat roof above. The tablecloth on the table outside was soaking wet and the rat droppings had melted into the fabric causing areas of brown stain.

Amelia stepped into the kitchen to find Geyta furiously polishing the surface of the kitchen table with fly spray. When questioned about what she was doing she simply explained :

"I do it with this and it stops the flies …."

She had sprayed it over food that hadn't been removed. Amelia didn't eat breakfast!

It was Amelia's last day with the family and Lucu said they could borrow his old car. They took up the offer and drove the country way down narrow lanes to Marsascala and then on to Marsasloxx. The fishing village was packed with locals who travelled distances to buy from the market. Despite the rain, the main street was swarming with people anxious to get their vegetables and fruit, or to simply look for a bargain on one of the many clothing outlets.

Amelia was aware that the car was belching out black smoke, but was a bit taken aback when a poser passenger in an open sports car stopped beside her in traffic, spat at her and shouted,

"Why don't you put your f****** car up your arse!"

Geyta didn't hear and even if she had, she wouldn't have reacted. Amelia was relieved that they were able to get back without the car breaking down. She handed the keys to Lucu and prepared to leave. Her flight was at 8pm so she needed to get to the airport fairly soon.

Lucu moved the position of the driver's seat and revved up the engine whilst he waited for Amelia to say her goodbyes to the family. Geyta wanted to go to the airport to see her best friend leave. There was a certain sadness in Amelia's heart because she knew she wouldn't be returning. This visit was purely one to tie up hanging threads. To tie up those lose ends that were never tied when she left before Michael all those years ago.

They hugged and kissed each other. This was a friendship birthed in adversity, but an honest loving friendship nevertheless.

Amelia shivered. The dying embers of her fire needed stoking. She reached to put on another log. Her tea was cold, again. She glanced at the clock. My goodness! She had been daydreaming for most of the day. She moved out of her chair and looked at the menu she had scribbled out for that day. The fish soup had already been prepared and she could accompany that with a dry quinoa biscuit.

Her recovery from her illness was steady and although she had been healed, she still did everything with forethought never wanting to get back to that disabling time.

The telephone rang. She reached to answer it.

"Hello Grandma! We finished school today. It's half-term! We are going to Cyprus tomorrow!"

After all those years of adventure and heartache, her life had, indeed, turned full circle! And, now her beloved son was to retrace her footsteps, but his journey would not be the same as hers!

It was time for another cup of Rooibos!